LURED: The Ulti

Chapter One
SOUTHBROOK

The year was 1662 and witch hunting had been on a world wide rise since the late 1650's. By July, ninety percent of the witches who lived in the hidden crooks of planet Earth had been dusted with salt to eliminate their powers, tied to trees with rope and set alight until their flesh sizzled away and instead became a pile of unholy ash.

A series of unfortunate events had taken place in Southbrook, England, a rural picturesque town where the majority of the small population were devout catholics. There had been a drought for a month, unexplainable fires and a rounded total of two hundred people reported missing by the end of August. The catholic people of Southbrook whispered to one another in the streets how it was the Lord who was responsible and that he was the one who had laid out these awful punishments, as a result of the lack of Catholicism within the town and youth becoming more rebellious with each new generation and birthing even more careless youth which were not educated by the bible. The non catholics in the town, however, we're leaning more to believe in the superstition of these events due to the large peak in witch hunting.

By the end of August, after two hundred catholic people who attended the Southbrook town church had gone missing, the devout catholics set torches alight and wandered the streets of the town, preaching words from their holy book and yelling how they would kill anybody who dared to not attend every Sunday mass at the Church from that point onwards.

A week later, it was time for Sunday mass at the Church. A damp smelling, cold, dusty looking church that was built in the mid 1400s. Sister Agnes Kirktrut, a harrowing seventy year old wrinkled, pale, blue eyed and grey haired nun that had been serving at the Church for fifty years, was standing by the entrance of the church holding a sheet of paper so that she could make a record of who had attended the mass. She made a separate list of those who did not attend written in red.

"Ha" she sniggers to Father Elliot Eastwood, the head priest of the Church. "Just look at this list of non - attendees. I don't think that they ever really realised that our words were those of the lord and the truth, plans will be swiftly arranged after mass" continues Agnes. Father Elliot nods his head, strolls his way up to the pulpit and brings the mass to an opening.

"Those who attended today, may you be blessed by the lord. Our religion is dying out, Just look at what has happened to our town. Only the lord could cast such heinous events upon us. The river banks, DRY! All these people, LOST!" Father Elliot cries. "Where are our people?! where is the sacred water that runs through this town?! WHERE?!" He then becomes too distressed to

3

continue with the speech, so he calls Sister Agnes to the pulpit to take over whilst he composes himself.

"Good morning. Thank goodness you all have attended, otherwise this list of people I'm sending over to Satan would be rather lengthy" says a sinister sounding Agnes whilst cracking her swollen arthritic knuckles and flashing her checklist to her audience. The audience's faces gain a concerned expression. Agnes continues, "very smart of you all to attend only when you're threatened with the knot in a rope. I pity you all. Look at you. Where are your morals? Where are your hearts? Where is the lord in your lives? You all disgust me. How could you not try your very hardest to keep the holy book running through your family? All your daughters and sons are now non - believers! What happened to this town being catholic! You should be ashamed! Well, at least you bothered to showed up today. Smart choice, as those who did not attend, I have on my list and you will hear their cries tomorrow. If you're lucky enough, you'll even hear their necks snap." Agnes giggles. Father Elliot returns to the pulpit, thanks everyone for attending and then dismisses them all.

The audience stand up and begin to exit the church in a stunning silence. Their blood has run cold, they're terrified of what will happen to their town and to their own families.

A small toddler tightly clutches his mother's hand and questions "mummy, will we be okay?" "Yes" his mother frantically replies whilst swallowing a ball in her throat. "We are moving away tomorrow, please begin to pack all of your clothes as soon as we get home." The young boy releases his mother's hand, sheds a tear and says that he doesn't want to leave. "Come now, we will be safer overseas. Your friends, if they're smart enough, will all come too. But there's no time for persuading, you will make more friends where we are heading. It is just no longer safe to live here" says his mother whilst shedding a tear. The young boy nods his head, once again clutches his mother's hand and walks alongside her.

 Back inside the church, Sister Agnes pulls Father Elliot aside and asks him to take a seat. Father Elliot slowly lowers himself to a cold, hard, stiff wooden chair.

 "I have counted. We will need enough rope for the fifty nine people that did not attend today, I have their names and addresses on my paper" says Agnes.

 "Well, are you sure about this? What if they're all correct. What if these events truly were witchcraft?" Expresses Father Elliot with a concerned tone.

 "Of course not. It is the lord's punishment. These atheists, they took away our water and crops for a whole month. They took away our families. The rope is only the beginning for them. After I'm done with them, they belong to Satan and I am just positive that they will rot in hell for eternity!" Says Agnes, becoming increasingly agitated.

"Then so be it, I suppose we will get the rope and go on a tour of the town tomorrow afternoon. They will be hung in the streets to be shamed publicly. Everyone will be so satisfied to watch these disgusting people come to their last breath" agrees Father Elliot. Agnes and Father Elliot stand, she reaches out her bony arm covered with a layer of loose flab and shakes his hand. They calmly leave the church with an evil smirk written across both of their faces.

Monday.

The hunt has begun.

"I SUMMON GEORGE SMITH TO THE DEVIL" shouts Sister Agnes passionately with evil gleaming in her eyes as she wanders down the cobbled streets of Southbrook checking off her list of people she will tie her rope around and hang from the trees. The first house she and her catholic mob, including Father Elliot, arrive to is number thirty-four Broxholme Road, the home of twenty - one year old George Smith.

After her constant shouting, there is no reply from the home. Agnes hands her lit torch to another member of the mob and decides to break down the door of the house. SMASH. Everyone covers their ears. The sound of the shattering glass pierces the eardrums of the surrounding people. She opens the door and enters with no fear holding her back, she is fully committed to the task she has set upon herself and will carry it out with no limitations. In the house there are no lights turned on, no noise, you could quite literally hear a pin drop. Agnes walks through the hallway with her black leather shoes tapping against the polished wooden floor and enters the dining room. She is welcomed by the sudden outburst of babies crying. She walks over to the drawers where the high pitched crying is coming from. Low and behold, there is a baby girl dressed in pink and a baby boy dressed in blue hidden behind the drawers, squashed against the wall. Agnes feels no mercy for the children and aggressively reaches down her long flabby arms to grab them. Out of nowhere, the mother of the children carefully and silently creeps up behind Agnes with a silver candle holder clutched in her hands fully prepared to cave in Agnes' skull. However, Agnes sees the mother's shadow on the surface of the drawers and turns her head faster than the speed of lightning. The woman is too stunned to react, all she can do is gasp. Then, BANG. Agnes punches the mother in the face and knocks her to the floor. Blood flows from her nose, however she is still conscious. She lays on the ground.

"LEAVE MY FAMILY ALONE, I ATTENDED YOUR MASS, BUT YOUR RELIGION HAS NO PLACE IN MY HOME" screams the helpless mother.

"YOUR SON HAD BEEN WARNED. HE DID NOT ATTEND SUNDAY MASS AND THEREFORE HIS NECK WILL BE SNAPPED" yells Agnes.

"WE DO NOT BELIEVE IN YOUR PATHETIC BOOK. THE WORLD WILL BE BETTER WHEN

CATHOLICISM DIES OUT COMPLETELY AND IS UNHEARD OF. THE WITCHES IN THIS TOWN ARE YOUR CONCERN. HANG THE WITCHES INSTEAD OF MY INNOCENT SON. THE RECENT HAPPENINGS IN THIS TOWN IS THEIR DOING. WE ARE INNOCENT PEOPLE!" Replies the mother. SMACK. Agnes punches her again, this time in the throat making it hard for the mother to breathe, she gasps for air. Her son, George, enters the room from the bottom of the staircase.

"I'M HERE. I AM THE ONE YOU'RE LOOKING FOR. DO WHATEVER YOU WISH TO ME. BUT DO NOT LAY A HAND ON MY MOTHER OR MY SIBLINGS" he passionately expresses, Agnes stomps over to him and drags him by his shirt into the street where the rest of the mob is waiting. The babies continue to cry out, the mother screams for help but help would not be found in this situation. George is now in the evil hands of the catholic mob. Whilst Agnes prepares the rope,

Father Elliot reads loudly, "George Smith, for all of your sins and for all of your lack of compassion for the lord our saviour, may you forever rot in the burning pits of hell' George's mother runs onto the street to stop her, but she is caught by other members of the mob and threatened by their lit torches. There are screams from every direction. People living in houses nearby rush into their gardens to see what is happening. George is instructed to climb to the branch on an oak tree in the street chosen by Agnes where he will take his final breath and meet his doom. Agnes instructs him to tie the rope around his neck and form a noose.

"Are there any last words?" She asks.

George replies, "I love you mother, I love my siblings too. Justice will be served for the witches in this town whom my life is being taken in the place of. Farewell world."

"JUMP!" Screams Agnes, with an evil grin on her face. He screams, jumps and instantly his neck is snapped. George is now dead, his lifeless body is hanging from a bloodied tree branch. His mother drops to her knees and releases an agonising cry. Sister Agnes and her mob walk away from the house and move onto their next victim, then the next, then the next.

Sister Agnes and her mob go all day, travelling from house to house, murdering many innocent people. When the final neck has been snapped and the trees are decorated with dead bodies like baubles on a Christmas tree. Agnes and her mob go back to the Southbrook town church to rest and pray to their lord that the people they have just sacrificed will go straight to the home of Satan.

"Lord we have sacrificed in your name. Send them all to hell and reward our city with your ever flowing sacred water and retrieve our lost loved ones" they all chant in unison. After their chanting, Father Elliot reaches out for Agnes' hand. She turns to look into his eyes, takes his hand and they pray five times together. "Have mercy lord. Protect us lord. Father they are gone now. You don't have to punish us or our town no more."

The following days after these sacrifices are filled with sorrow, grief and anger from the families of those who had been sacrificed by Sister Agnes and her mob. Riots break out onto the street, the church is vandalised, but Sister Agnes stays in the sacristy of the church, behind a locked door, praying that those whose bodies are still hanging from the trees will be handed over to Satan. She feels no remorse, no guilt, no mercy for the families. Just pure evil towards these people.

The following Sunday after the sacrifices, mass at the Southbrook town Church goes ahead as normal. Many people from the town attend because they are still scared that if they do not, they will be thrown into the same ordeal they have watched loved ones go through so recently. So they sit paralysed and listen to Sister Agnes and Father Elliot read their holy scriptures. The audience leaves the church after mass, Agnes and Father Elliot stay behind. Agnes strolls to the nave of the church and kneels down to pray. Suddenly she hears a piercingly loud scream in her left ear. She jumps up and yells. Father Elliot hear's Agnes' scream from the chapel area of the church and runs over to her. She asks Father Elliot if he heard anything, yet to him this high pitched screech was inaudible. He did not hear a thing. He tells Agnes that she is just tired and that she should just go and rest for a while. So, she follows Father Elliot's instructions. She leaves the church and goes back to the nunnery.

Chapter Two
STRANGE HAPPENINGS

 The nunnery where Agnes lives is a couple of blocks
away from Webber Alley where supposedly three sister
witches lived. They are not genetically sisters, but many
years ago they performed a ceremony in which they used
a razor blade to slit a pentagram in each others wrists
and then smear their blood into each other's cuts in order
to become a sisterhood. These witches had been reported
and named in an old newspaper, they were forty five
year old Edith Knowles, thirty nine year old Rose
Cartwright and fifty six year old Mary Dwendle. They
were thought to be living from the blood of young
virgins. They would stalk their prey, abduct them and
then bring them back to their home in order to strap them
to a wooden chair, amputate their limbs with a saw and
then extract their blood into glass bottles to drink. They
would drink the blood because it was believed to make
them live longer and keep them looking youthful. Edith
was a short, larger lady with long brown hair and hazel
green eyes. Rose was a fair skinned, strawberry - blonde
haired, blue eyed, freckled, tall witch. Lastly, Mary had
short black hair, grey eyes and always wore a pair of
leather gloves. Strange things had happened in their area.
Many people who came into contact with these witches
became missing people, any animals that stepped onto
their lawn died a few days later and every so often there

would be an enormous cloud of ash in the skies above their house. So eventually, people stopped making an effort to hunt them down because they were afraid these witches were too powerful.

There had been numerous complaints about these witches to the Southbrook town Church, however Sister Agnes only believed that anything supernatural was the lord letting the world know that he was around. March 1660, there was an incident where a fellow nun from the church, Sister Martha, had gone over to the witch's' house to ask why some flowers from the nunnery garden had been stolen and planted in their lawn. It was Rose Cartwright who answered the door and simply told her to be excused because she was too busy for questions. After this encounter, the nun was found in her rocking chair in her bedroom with a slit throat and her own eyeballs placed in her mouth at one o'clock in the morning by another fellow nun going to check on her. It was a tragedy in the town as Sister Martha was well known in the community for being a kind and cheerful lady. But Sister Agnes didn't believe anything other than the words she read in the bible. She believed that Sister Martha had been slacking with her church duties and so it was the lord's way of punishing her. Because of Sister Agnes' claims, no investigations of a murder were ever carried out.

Agnes goes home, she lays down in her old four post bed covered by her strained sheets that hadn't been washed in decades. She experiences a sharp pain in her head and a frequent screeching noise in her left ear. Could it be the witches beginning to torture Sister Agnes? She lays, tossing and turning, fluffing her pillow because she just can't seem to get comfortable. She eventually can't handle the distress no more, so she drags herself out of bed feeling rather dead herself. She enters her kitchen and goes to brew herself a cup of English breakfast tea to see if it can help her to relax. Agnes boils some hot water and turns to grab a tea bag. The fire under where she is boiling her water in a saucepan suddenly gets whooshed by a freak gust of wind, meanwhile Agnes hears an audible breathy blow in her left ear, like there was a human stood right next to her. She swiftly twists around to see that the fire has gone out. With a concerned look on her face she travels to every door in her home to see if one is unlocked and rule out the possibility of any intruders.

"SHOW YOURSELF!" Agnes screams whilst running to her main entrance. "SHOW YOURSELF NOW!" she continues. Agnes checks all the doors in her putrid smelling, dust filled home and nobody is to be found. She scratches her forehead in confusion and convinces herself that the lord had came around to comfort her and blowing out the fire was his way of letting her know he was around. All the doors and widows were locked. Agnes returns to her bed, discarding the tea she was going to make, and falls into a deep sleep.

"AWFUL FOOL. YOUR MOUTH WILL DROOL, AFTER YOUR TONGUE IS CHOPPED AND YOUR FLOOR WILL BE MOPPED WITH YOUR BLOOD." Agnes quickly wakes up and hears these words being chanted in a demonic voice over and over in her home, so loudly she cannot bear it and has to cover her ears tightly. With her hands over her ears and a scrunched up face, Agnes runs about her home trying to find where this chanting is coming from. She goes right and up the stairs, turns left and enters the bathroom, there's nothing. She runs back down the freaking stairs and turns left into her living room, where a vase that she had resting on her dining table had been thrown and shattered against the wall.

"Oh my" Agnes says in concern. "What on earth is happening to me." Agnus feels drowsy and collapses on her hard, wooden floor.

The next day, Agnus awakes, prepares herself for the day ahead and sweeps up the shards of glass from her shattered glass.

"Thank you Lord for your protection. I know it is only YOU whom is welcomed into my home, therefore it was you who smashed my vase and put out the fire. Oh dear heavenly lord thank you for your visit" mumbles a delusional Agnes under her breath as she is on her knees sweeping up the glass.

She arrives at the Southbrook City Church and rushes over to Father Elliot who is sat reading his scriptures in a normal daily routine.

"Oh my, Father you would never be able to imagine the purity and content I am feeling this morning." Says Agnes.

"Why?" asks Father Elliot.

"He came to visit me, he knows that we all did good. We got rid of the dirt and grime that festered this City with their non belief. He came to thank me. I tried to make a tea but he blew out the fire, he even smashed my glass vase to let me know he was there. Oh father how great it feels to know he is here."

Father Elliot closes and rests his bible on his knees. "How incredible. Did anything else happen, Agnes?." he questions.

"Well, yes, there was something else rather strange. Changing, awfully loud chanting. It would not stop. The screaming is still on my ears. It was the strangest thing." relays Agnes.

"Agnes I am very frightened to say that I experienced the very same encounter. I went to bed last night, woke up with the screaming in my ears of a very unholy chant. I could not figure out what it was" says Father Elliot. "AWFUL FOOL. YOUR MOUTH WILL DROOL, AFTER YOUR TONGUE IS CHOPPED AND YOUR FLOOR WILL BE MOPPED WITH YOUR BLOOD" they mutter in unison. Father Elliot and Agnes stare into each others eyes in disbelief. Father Elliot's bible falls from his knees and thuds on the floor. The church door slams shut, they both turn their heads fast to look, then behind them they hear female voices sniggering, they turn their heads again the other way. All the candles blow out with yet another freak gust of wind.

"How do we explain this Agnes? Is it witchcraft?" Questions a fearful Father Elliot.

"Rubbish. Only the lord can summon us, witchcraft is ricocheted by our religion. The lord would never let such things take place in our lives. It is likely the lord again, coming to us both now, again to thank us" Agnes reassures Father Elliot. "Those witches, who lived a few blocks away from you in Webber Alley. Do they still live there, Agnes?" asks Father Elliot.

"Well, I'm not really certain. But I can check, tonight, when the moon arises I will go to the house and peep through the windows. But what good is this information Father?" Asks Agnes. "Well, if they're still hovering around with their bottles of blood and pentagrams, then they could very well have something to do with all of this, Agnes." Says Father Elliot.

"Well, if they are caught during any of their rituals, or putting their magic in the way of the church and our lord, then they will be executed. But Father I don't think we have a thing to worry about. These witches can do anything they please to the rest of the people, so long as those who attend the church are safe. Which they will be.

Those who attend church are protected by our lord. So we don't have nothing to worry about" reassures Agnes.

Chapter Three
MEET THE WITCHES

The following evening Sister Agnes sits on her doorstep eating an oxtail and potato stew, waiting for the moon to appear. When darkness falls, she will set out on her mission to try and catch the witches. She chews her last potato and looks up to the sky, "ahhh" she gasps, "it is time." The moon has appeared, it is 7PM and darkness has arrived. It is time for Agnes to go to Webber Alley and see if the witches are home. She locks her door and begins to walk to the end of Yielders Close, she then turns onto Windet Avenue and walks a mile past two blocks. She gets to the third block, which is where Webber Alley, the road of the witches is. She turns onto the Alley and strolls up to the house. Firstly, she hears voices. Female voices. Cackling. Similar to the voices her and Father Elliot has heard in the church. Agnes hides behind a wall with her head peeking over so she can get a clear view of the house. All the rooms were in darkness, until suddenly there is a flash of blue light in one of the rooms upstairs, followed by chanting. "Oh my" mumbles Sister Agnes with a concerned tone. "Whatever could they be doing in there?" she questions herself. SLAM. Agnes hears a door slam shut from the outside of the home, she lowers her head under the wall but still with her eyes level with the home so that she can see everything. A tall, fair - skinned, strawberry - blonde haired lady wearing a petticoat, waistcoat and apron walks out of a door at the back of the house holding something rather awful, it was Rose Cartwright, one of the witches. It appears to be that she is holding a carcass, Agnes was unsure whether it belonged to an animal, or a human being. A set of ribs covered in blood and gunge. Rose begins to dig up a whole in the mud in her garden, before planting the ribs and covering them up. She goes back inside the house, Agnes stands to get a clearer view of what is going on. BANG. Rose, once again, slams the door and returns. Agnes ducks down again but is almost certain that she had locked eyes with Rose for a split second, her heart begins to palpitate and everything starts to feel that little bit more real. Agnes swallows loudly in fear. She raises her head again to see what is going on, Rose is no longer looking. Agnes sees what seems to be a human head, the head of a young lady with long blonde hair, again being planted into a hole in the mud. Agnes can't help but gip as she is going to be sick and is now more afraid than ever that she has been spotted by the witch.

 Agnes runs. She runs fast. She gets back onto Windet Avenue, turns the corner and then she suddenly collapses. Agnes is out of breath and tired from running, she can't pull herself up from the ground, but not only because she is breathless, but because she physically cannot lift herself up. It appears that Sister Agnus has been put under a spell, her whole body is frozen and she cannot scream for help no matter how hard she tries. On Windet Avenue lays a seventy year old nun who is completely paralysed. It is night time and everybody else is asleep, no help is available. Then, there is a flash of light before her eyes.

"Oh Lord, thank goodness you're here, you came to save me. Oh lord I thank you." Agnes whimpers inside her delusional mind.

"THE LORD ISN'T AVAILABLE RIGHT NOW" screams Rose, now stood in front of Agnes with Mary and Edith holding lit torches. Rose clicks her fingers and now Agnes can talk, but only with a gentle whisper so that she cannot shout for help. Rose bends down in her petticoat and apron with her flowing strawberry blonde hair brushing against Agnes' face, to hear what Agnes is saying.

"The lord will punish you" Agnes laughs. "Do you really think you will get away with this in the final judgement? Paralysing an elderly lady on the streets and harassing her! You're not even going to go to purgatory, straight to hell!" She continues. SNAP. Rose snaps her fingers and Agnes can no longer speak, her, Mary and Edith lift Agnes from the ground and carry her to their home. They enter through the front grand entrance. Agnes is greeted by other younger witches. This grand house is now a Coven. Due to the witch hunting and rise in numbers of deaths it had been converted by the three sister witches into a safe haven for the remaining witches in the town to hide from the catholic predators. In total there were only twelve witches remaining in the town, now all living under this one roof for protection. The walls are painted black, it is infested with cobwebs, the walls are decorated with hand painted pentagrams and satanic figures, the first sight is the large hallway, then connecting to the grand and recently polished wooden staircase.

"Is this the one?" asks Juliet Martin, a younger beginner witch. "The one who carried out her pathetic routine to murder half of this city because she thought it was them who caused the droughts and everything else that happened? HA!" Laughs Juliet to Rose. "Well I have news for you, Sister" now talking to Agnes. "It was I and my fellow witches who caused these events. The lord is your saviour, well where is he now? Where is his protection now, huh? Nowhere to be found. You and your people have been executing our kind for years now. Witch hunting? when did that become a sport? Now I think it's time we did some catholic hunting. Am I correct ladies?" she asks her fellow witches. "Ha!" they all laugh in reply.

Rose speaks "Yes. Agnes, you and your catholic people have killed almost half of our kind, and for what? is there an excuse for this? Our religion is what the world needs. Magic. Nobody needs to lord when you can click your fingers and have whatever you need, correct? People like you have been tearing us down from the start. Now you think it was the Lord who caused the droughts and sent three thousand people missing? Well, wrong. It was us. All of us. The best part about being a witch is that you can do anything you please and nobody knows who it was, so I guess it's only right that you blamed your lord for these happenings. But no, it was us, how pathetic do you feel now?"

Rose clicks her fingers and Agnes is now able to speak normally. "WITCHES! IT WAS ALL OF YOU WHO BROKE INTO MY HOME AND SMASHED MY VASE, IT WAS YOU WHO PUT OUT THE FIRE, IT WAS YOU WHO SNIGGERED AT ME IN THE CHURCH. OH LORD, WHY HAVE I BEEN SO BLIND?" cries out Agnes.

"Well, it's too late now" replies Edith. "You have been blind, extremely blind, it was us who caused these tragic events, we sent those who punished us for our religion into the forest to die and we figured that letting this town run dry for a month would maybe teach some more of you a lesson. But the witch hunts continued, so now we will have a voice, and madam we will use you as our ammunition for the church to put an end to this witch hunting once and for all. They either give us our peace or their throats will be slit, just like what happened to Sister Martha last March when she stepped onto our lawn" continues Edith. "Oh lord, why has this happened to me. I have served you all of my life and I am now in the impure hands of these non believers. Lord show me the way" prays Agnes. SLAP. Rose slaps Agnes and instructs the rest of the witches to grab her and disrobe her.

Chapter Four
LITTLE BOY EDWARD IS FOR DINNER

"STRIP THESE HOLY GARMENTS OFF OF HER!"
She shouts. Juliet, Mary and Edith all grab Agnes as she
cries for help, they strip her of her habit and veil, they
also rip away the wooden crucifix necklace from around
her neck so forcefully that it slits her skin, causing blood
to trickle down Agnes' neck and all over her décolletage.
Blood continues to drip from Agnes while she is laid
naked on the wooden panel ground in the hallway of the
coven. "Nobody will find you now, Agnes" says Juliet.
"You're our property. You belong to US! Mary is
clairvoyant, she knows that 'Father Elliot' knew that you
were coming to see us tonight. He will more than likely
come looking for you tomorrow, that is when he will
have to put an end to this witch hunting, or alternatively,
your throat will be slit" she continues. Edith drags Agnes
by her bloodied neck into their dining room. She pulls
out a butchers knife from the top drawer.

"This is what will send you STRAIGHT to your lord
tomorrow if Father Elliot carries on trying to hunt us
down. Ladies, take her to her room" she says angrily.
"My room?" Agnes asks timidly. "Yes, I am sure that
you will be very comfortable there."
Juliet, Mary and Rose drag Agnes up three flights of
stairs to her room, whilst other members of the coven on
each floor of the house stand and watch with smiles on

their faces. Mary pulls out a key from her apron and unlocks the door, inside it is the room that only a prisoner would be familiar with. Thick with dust, one small candle being her only source of light, a single blanket laid on the ground and a bowl for her to ... release herself into. They throw her in and lock the door as Agnes cries and screams for help. Mary shouts down the grand staircase to Rose who is on ground floor "SHE HAS BEEN PUT AWAY!"

Rose replies "Good, now let the torture begin tomorrow morning before Father Elliot's visit" with a large smirk on her face.

The witches walk downstairs and collect up off of the floor Agnes' clothing and belongings that they stripped her of. They hide her bible in a cupboard in the living room and burn her holy garments by chucking them onto the fireplace. As her clothes burn, the witches watch and cackle. They then sit in a circle and produce plans of how they will torment Agnes throughout the night and how they will threaten Father Elliot if he should come to search for Agnes tomorrow.

"Should we make her eat some of dear little boy Edward's flesh?" asks Juliet. Poor Edward was a thirteen year old virgin boy whom they had previously brutally murdered in order to drink his blood for vitality and youth.

"Excellent idea! His meat is close to expiration anyway. I am sure that she would enjoy a nice steaming bowl of Edward's stew" replies Rose, grinning widely.

Nighttime falls. Rose is stood in the kitchen in her black silk negligee peeling some potatoes, carrots and cabbage, fresh from their garden, ready to prepare and cook the stew. She opens up her thick, dusty recipe book to page 67 and it reads:

VIRGIN VITALITY CHUNKY FLESH AND VEGETABLE STEW

Ingredients:
10 Potatoes
10 Carrots
1 Whole Cabbage
1kg of Fresh Flesh
Bones for broth
Pint of blood for sauce

Method:
Peel and chop the potatoes and carrots.
Chop the cabbage, any maggots a bonus!
Boil vegetables.
Add to deep tin with chunky flesh, bone broth and blood sauce.
Put in the oven for around an hour.

"Edith, go and get Edward's flesh from the ice bath" instructs Rose. Edith nods towards Rose before exiting the room and sprinting up the stairs to the bathroom on the first floor where little boy Edward's flesh lies in a bathtub, preserved delicately with a surrounding of cubed ice. Edith reaches into the foul bathtub, crunching her hands through the small cubes of ice, before squelching the rubber - like, bloody and fresh smelling human flesh. She lifts out some fleshy off cuts of Edward's arms and legs and transfers it into a medium sized wooden barrel kept in the room, again covering the flesh with ice to keep it as fresh and tender as possible. She carries the barrel of flesh with both hands back down the stairs to take to the kitchen for Rose to slice into chunks and stew in the oven with her freshly prepared vegetables.

"Perfect" says Rose.

"This meat is perfectly tender and fresh. I just need to let it slightly settle to room temperature to ensure the best quality! Then about an hour in the oven and little boy Edward should be beautifully tender. Just like our skin will be after drinking all of his virgin blood" she brags. CHOP. CHOP. CHOP. Rose cuts little boy Edward's flesh into chunks with her large, freshly sharpened butcher's knife like it is fresh poultry. The smell is putrid. After she has finished slicing the slimy flesh, she wipes the knife clean on her negligee and combines the flesh with the boiled vegetables in a deep roasting tray, then creates a mixture consisting of Edward's blood with some of Edward's bone which she had prepared earlier on in the day to make a rich sauce. She then leaves the stew to cook for around an hour.

An hour passes and the stew is ready, Rose opens up the oven door to release the foul smell of roasted human flesh.

"Ahhhh" she says blissfully as she sniffs the steam coming from the oven, "Smells delicious" she adds. She plates up the stew for all the fellow witches to enjoy, and one for Sister Agnes to gip upon. "LADIES, STEW IS READY" she shouts. The witches come downstairs to eat their stew.

"Oh my, how stunning" Mary comments on the stew.

"Enjoy" says Rose to the ladies as they all take their first bite.

"Delicious" says Juliet.

"It has a wonderful flavour. Now, maid, would you be ever so kind and take up a bowl to your new bible buddy Agnes?" Sniggers Rose.

"I would be more than happy to do so, Madam" replies Fiona, the maid. Fiona is a sixty two year old German catholic lady, whom Rose had also kidnapped, but to act as a slave for the witches, tending to their every need.

Chapter Five
AGNES MEETS ONE OF HER OWN KIND

Rose hands the bowl to Fiona, she grabs it and then swiftly makes her way up to the first floor where Agnes' room is. Fiona gets the shivers before knocking on the door. KNOCK KNOCK. Fiona knocks on to the door and steps back awaiting a response.

"What do you want, evil satanist?" Growls an aggressive sounding Agnes.

"It is actually me, Fiona, the maid" says Fiona as she unlocks the door and enters to see Agnes, laid naked.

"Oh my goodness" Fiona gasps.

"This is just like what happened to me" she says, shedding a tear.

"Whatever do you mean?" Questions Agnes. Fiona walks over to where Agnes is laid and kneels beside her on the floor.

"Well, I am one of you. I love the Lord too. Or at least I did, but my faith certainly has been tested in this hell hole. Rose kidnapped me too, because I was an easy target I suppose, a vulnerable old and kind catholic lady, like yourself I presume. She told me that she was hosting a bible club, every Tuesday at four o'clock in the afternoon and that she would love for me to attend. So, like a fool and with no guidance from the lord, I came to this place with my bible fully willing to spread the good word of the lord. But then before I could even say hello,

I was dragged by my vail into the middle of the hallway. I laid screaming being pinned to the ground by Rose and being stripped of my holy garments by Edith and Mary, before being carried up the stairs and thrown into this very same room. Rose then decided that she could use some help around the house with the cooking and cleaning, so she turned me into a slave and that is exactly what I am to this day, two years later" explains Fiona. Agnes' eyes bulge.

"Well, can you stay in here with me? Maybe we can think of a way to get out of this place" questions Agnes.

"I am afraid I cannot. I live up on the third floor, in the maid's quarters. You may see me around the house though, cleaning and cooking, if they do let you out of this room that is" replies Fiona.

"What do you mean, if they do let me out of this room?" Asks Agnes.

"Well, I have no idea of what they are going to do to you. They already have one maid, I'm sure that they do not need another" replies Fiona.

"Well, Rose mentioned that she was going to use me, sort of as a pawn, because I am the head nun at the Southbrook town church see. So, I have a lot of power and she wants to use me against Father Elliot. She wants him to come and look for me so that she can threaten him with the ultimatum of either taking me back and putting an end to the witch hunting or him deciding that witch hunting will continue but that would sentence me to death" says Agnes.

"Well, let's hope that he doesn't go with the latter then. Anyway, I must go. I will get into trouble if Rose or anybody else hears or sees me being nice to you. I will go and clean" says Fiona.

Agnes picks up her fork and stabs it into the flesh and before Fiona can say anything, Agnes inserts the chunk of human flesh into her mouth. SPLATTER, SPLATTER, SPLATTER. Agnes drops her fork to the ground and is sick all over her naked body.

"GOOD LORD, WHAT ON EARTH IS THAT?!" Shouts Agnes with sick drooling down her chin.

"I was actually just about to say, I wouldn't eat that if I was you" replies Fiona. Meanwhile, down in the kitchen, Rose hears Agnes' puking and shouting, so she grins and frolics up the stairs into the room. Fiona stands up and pulls a cloth out from her apron and faces the wall as if she is cleaning as soon as she hears the door creek open.

"What is going on here? Huh?" Questions Rose.

"Nothing Rose. I am just doing some dusting. Agnes is elderly, the dust could be bad for her" replies Fiona.

"SILENCE SLAVE. I wasn't talking to you" bellows Rose. Fiona drops her cloth in fright but bends down to pick it back up and continue to polish the wall.

"Well, if you cannot tell, satanist, I was just sick all over myself because of this hideous stew" says Agnes to Rose. Rose looks at Agnes and responds

"Sweet Agnes, how would you ever know if you like something or not if you have only tried it once? EAT IT!" Shouts Rose.

"I will NOT eat this foul stew!" Screeches Agnes. Rose huffs, walks over to Agnes, grabs her tightly by her hair and plunges her face into the bloody stew. The stew splashes out onto the floor and Agnes tries to scream but is suffocating. Rose holds her head in the stew for a whole thirty seconds before letting Agnes come up for air. She finally releases Agnes. GASP. Agnes is blue in colour and gasping for air.

"You almost killed me!" Shouts a breathless Agnes.

"You won't be so lucky to survive next time if you continue to disobey my orders" replies Rose.

"FIONA! Get out of here. Pick Agnes' bowl up to clean" she continues as Agnes lays on the floor feeling frail.

"Of course, madam" replies Fiona, picking up Agnes' plate and skipping out of the room in terror. Rose steps out of the room and slams the door shut.

Agnes is now alone in her room, feeling more hopeless in her faith than ever. She prays to the Lord that she will be set free. Naked and soaked in her own stinking, green vomit, Agnes kneels down on the creaky wooden floor to pray.

"Oh Lord, let this be over. I served you all my life, why am I being punished? Why would this awful unblessed food enter my body? Why would I be being held here, naked, alone? Lord show me a sign that you are here and it will be enough for me to hope for my day of release from this hostility" prays a blubbering Agnes.

Chapter Six
BLOOD BATH

Agnes has been laying on the floor covered in her own spew for hours now. She decides she must stand back up straight otherwise her old body will lock into her lying position. She slowly climbs back up but can't hold her urine. She urinates all over her naked body.

"HELP!" Shouts Agnes, now covered in her own vomit and urine. "I NEED TO GO TO CLEAN MYSELF" she continues. Rose hears her cries for help from downstairs, she snaps her fingers and is teleported into Agnes' room faster than the speed of lightning.

"Look at you. Soaked in your own bodily fluids. Aren't you pathetic" she comments staring at Agnes' naked body.

"Please" blubbers Agnes. "I really must clean myself, I won't pull any tricks. Please just show me to the bathroom" she pleads.

"That sounds fair to me. To be completely truthful, I was planning a nice bath for you anyway" says Rose. "I shall go and prepare it for you right now" she continues.

Rose locks the door, smirks to herself and frolics down the stairs to the kitchen. She goes to the sink, where it is filled with young virgin boy Edward's blood. "I'm sure we can spare some" whispers Rose to herself. She grabs a vase from the kitchen table and fills it with the thick, crimson red blood.

"Ha" she says to herself as she turns around and begins to walk back up to the stairs. "Agnes is going to be smelling beautifully" she cackles. Rose goes to the bathroom and pours out the blood from the vase into the small bath tub. The sound is awful, as if little boy Edward was hanging from the roof with his blood splattering from his amputated limbs. Rose sighs with satisfaction. She goes across the corridor to Agnes' room and unlocks the door.

"Your bath has been prepared, follow me" instructs Rose. Agnes follows Rose in a trail of her elegant poise and long flowing strawberry - blonde hair. They enter the bathroom and Agnes lets out an almighty screech.

"WHAT IN THE WORLD IS THIS?" questions a distressed Agnes.

"This, Agnes, is just some leftover ingredients from the stew that you ate earlier. Did you ever wonder what kind of meat was in the stew? Well, I can happily inform you that it was the meat extracted from the same body as where this blood came from" explains Rose.

"Body?" questions a now distressed and fearful Agnes.

"Yes, poor little catholic boy Edward. He was only thirteen, a boy of the church and well, sadly for his family I'm sure, he was the first pure one we could get our hands on. We amputated his limbs and extracted the blood for us witches to enjoy the youthful benefits of. However his meat was rather tasty too" says Rose licking her lips. The colour drains out of Agnes' body.

She is blue. She now becomes extremely angry and agitated.

"HOW DARE YOU. I KNOW EDWARD. AND I KNOW HIS FAMILY, EDWARD, THE LITTLE ALTAR BOY AT THE CHURCH" shouts Agnes. "Well, you KNEW him" laughs Rose.

"DO NOT SPEAK, FOUL SATANIST. AN INNOCENT LITTLE BOY, SLICED APART AND FED TO ME. OH YOU ARE JUST WAITING ON THE LORD'S WRATH. YOU AND YOUR SISTERS HAVE HEFTY PUNISHMENTS COMING YOUR WAY!" screams Agnes. Rose grabs Sister Agnes' arm, Agnes screams in agony, Rose twists it as far as she can behind Agnes' back and calls for Mary.

"MARY!" shouts Rose.

"Come and help me bathe Agnes" she continues. Mary here's Rose's screeches and runs up the three flights of stairs to the bathroom.

"I have her arm, you lift her by her legs, we are going to drop her into this bathtub filled with little boy Edward's blood" instructs Rose to Mary.

"ROSE! This is ludacris! Really! Little boy Edward's fresh blood is supposed to be for us to bathe in and drink for our youthfulness! Why would you be so kind to Agnes?!" shouts Mary.

"FOOL! Do you think Catholics enjoy bathing in their own people's blood? This is no treat for her. But a punishment. She will be bathed in the blood and then put

37

to bed so that we can make the plans for tomorrow morning." says Rose in an aggressive fashion. Mary lifts Agnes' seventy year old legs and they both drop her into the blood. Agnes screams "OH, THE SMELL, I CANNOT STAND THIS, OH EDWARD, THE LORD WILL TAKE YOU. THESE WITCHES, THESE AWFUL AWFUL WITCHES. I AM SO SORRY." She lays there. Rose and Mary take great pleasure over bathing Agnes in Edward's blood. They hover over the bathtub grinning whilst splashing Agnes' naked body with the crimson red blood. SPLASH SPLASH SPLASH. They splash it over Agnes' face, they wash her hair in it. It stains her fair grey hair with a tinge of red.

"OH WHAT TORTURE" screams Agnes, squirming and struggling as Mary and Rose are restraining her.

"Yes, catholic fool. If you get joy from burning all of us witches, then you can for sure enough appreciate bathing in the blood of your own people" says Rose.

"Okay, I think that should be enough. I can no longer bare the smell, let's lock her back in her cage" Rose says to Mary. Mary grabs Agnes' legs whilst Rose grabs her arms once again, they swing her out of the bathtub onto the wooden floor. Agnus lays slithering on the floor, slimy with blood, whimpering. Rose and Mary lift her and carry her to her room. They throw her in and lock the door.

Mary and Rose turn to go back down the stairs. Mary grabs onto Rose's arm, Rose turns to her, they lock eyes and Rose is surprised that Mary would touch her in such an aggressive way.

"That blood is supposed to be for US. All of us! Now there is barely enough for us all! Did you not think to consult the rest of us living in this place before such a selfish act? It's no surprise, actually. You have always been so self - centred and selfish and I'm so sick of you and your ordering people around. Just stay out of my way" expresses an agitated Mary.

Rose's fair skin blushes and she stumbles on her words "g-g-g- GO AWAY! Get out of my sight. How dare you speak to me like this!" she manages to say.

"OH there we go again! Demands, demands, demands. You always think you're the boss in this place, that you're in charge, just because you're the prettiest and you use your looks to seduce all the men in this city. Like the flower that you're named after, you're pretty at first sight, but then you notice the thorns and it makes the flower seem so much uglier. You're no more important than the rest of us in this coven, Rose. You're not special. Just remember it was actually me and Edith who got you here in the first place" Mary replies. She brushes past Rose and walks down the stairs in front of her. Rose stays still, she is shocked. She isn't used to this treatment.

Chapter Seven
EVERY ROSE HAS IT'S THORN

Rose is a descendent of the well known family, the Cartwrights. Back in the late fifteen hundreds, when it was even more so forbidden to be a witch. Rose's grandparents were the talk of the city when after a heated argument about their child (Rose's mother) and their differences in parenting. Rose's grandmother, Elizabeth Cartwright, for the first time exposed that she was a witch and out of rage used her powers to boil her husband, Henry Cartwright's blood until steam spurted out from his ears and he died. Elizabeth always knew that she was a witch but kept her powers hidden from her husband and family all her life because she knew that if she were to be exposed as a witch that she would be burnt at the stake. Which, is exactly what happened. Days after the murder, Elizabeth was arrested after being exposed for using her powers to boil her husband's blood. She was sprinkled with salt to weaken her powers to the point that they barely work and then was tied to a tree and burnt. Rose's mother, Eden Cartwright, was only four years old when this happened. After the death of both her parents, she was sent to live with another family who wanted to adopt a young girl. The family who adopted Eden were extremely rich, her adoptive mother was actually a distant cousin of Queen Elizabeth I. Eden had a great upbringing with her new family.

Then, when Eden was twenty three years old, she fell in love with a German man. Eden left her family to live with him in Germany, they lived there for four years. Then when Eden became pregnant they decided to move back to Southbrook in England where the child would have a better life. Eden gave birth to her daughter, Rose, in the Johnson Hospital. She decided to give her her surname, Cartwright. Rose Cartwright was born. However, Eden became severely ill after the birth of Rose and passed away within just a few months of having complications. Rose then lived alone with her father and for a few years it was all fantastic. Then her father lost his job and money became an issue, he became and alcohol and started to sexually abuse Rose. She was just a child and he treated her so inappropriately. Rose suffered this abhorrent treatment for the rest of the time that she lived with him. When Rose was just nineteen years old she discovered that she had some sort of powers. Her mother, Eden, was never a witch. The genetics had skipped a generation. Rose had inherited the magical genes from her grandmother.

One night when Rose was laid in bed, her pervert of a father came into her room demanding her to disrobe herself. The more Rose said no, the more her father became increasingly aggressive. He eventually decided to just rip off her clothes and try to penetrate her. Rose squirmed and laid screaming and feeling so weak until all of a sudden something clicked in her head and she decided that she needed to gain control, so she closed her eyes tightly and wished her father would go away. She wished for him to stop, for him to be paralysed so he could no longer abuse her. After she wished this, her father froze and dropped onto her as if he were just a lifeless corpse. Rose screamed and pulled the body off of her, it was then that she realised he was still breathing and his monstrous eyes were still wide open. She brought her face closer to his mouth, holding her nose so she couldn't smell his whiskey breath, and heard ever so gentle breathing. Her father was indeed still alive, but not at all moving, or making a single sound apart from his gentle breathing. It seemed that Rose's wish had come true, he was now paralysed from head to toe. She laughed in his face and did a celebratory dance. Then paused with the realisation that she now had magical powers.

"Woah!" She says to herself. "This could be useful" she giggles. She grabs her father and seats him in a chair, fear is now visible in his eyes. Rose goes to the kitchen to grab a butchers knife, she returns to her room where her father is sat up straight in the chair.

"For all these years, every day that you have touched me and made me cry myself to sleep. I will slit you with this knife every day until you die" she strongly weeps to her father. She swings the knife and slashes her father's arm. Blood gushes from his arm whilst Rose sits on her bed and psychotically laughs. She feeds him and puts fluid into her father's body every day to keep him alive just so that she can torture him. One day, when Rose sets out into the city, she comes across an old, large rusted building. Rose becomes intrigued and goes inside. It is Mary Dwendle and Edith Knowles who immediately come to her. "Who are you?" asks a nervous Rose to Mary and Edith.

"Well, for a better question, who are you?" replies Mary.

"Rose, Rose Cartwright" says Rose, with a trembling voice.

Mary and Edith both look at each other in astonishment. "She's here. The third sister! She has finally found her way!" Says an excited Edith.

"My… way? What is going on here?" Replies Rose.

"Come with us, dear, let us all have a little chat" says Mary, holding out her hand for Rose to hold as she brings her into a sitting room. Mary and Edith sit, Rose sits in front of them.

"Rose, Rose Rose Rose. We have been waiting for you to find your way to us. Welcome to the sisterhood. You are a witch" says Mary.

"Oh goodness, now it all makes sense, the powers, these strange feelings I've been having" says Rose.

"Yes, you're a Cartwright. From the famous Cartwright family. Your grandmother was a witch, she boiled your grandfather alive" says Edith.

"Oh, well, where is my grandmother now?" asks Rose.

"Well, she was a witch, people found out what she had done and they burned her at the stake" explains Mary.

"Oh goodness, how awful, so, wait a second. We are witches! Will we not get the same treatment now?" asks a frightened Rose.

"Not if were careful my dear, only witches know that they are witches. We don't look any different from anybody else. Unless we use our powers in public nobody will ever know. Which is why we are a sisterhood. We need to stick together." Says Mary. "Yes" agrees Edith showing off the pentagram shaped scar on her arm.

"Me and Mary have these. You're the third sister so you will be given one of these now. We engrave a pentagram into your skin, me and Mary will cut ours open again and we all allow each others blood to flow into our own blood stream. So in that special way, we are connected by blood." Edith continues. Rose comes to realise that this is her life now and that she must take the appropriate steps to honour who she is. So, she agrees to go through with the initiation ceremony. Edith and Mary are her sisters and they will spend their lives together, practicing their powers. Mary pulls out a blade from her apron and traces around her own pentagram scar. Blood pours onto the floor as she hisses in pain. She then does the same to Edith. Then Mary carefully marks the pentagram symbol onto Rose's arm. Rose screams in agony. Edith has to hold her down so that she cannot wriggle around in her chair. After all their pentagrams are gaping open, they take it in turns to rub their arms together, moaning as if it were a sexual act. They then patch up their wounds with cloth and rope until it stops bleeding. They now all have their pentagram scars on their arms. Rose is officially a part of the sisterhood.

Years go by and Rose decides to move into the coven on Webber Alley so that she can strengthen her skills and stay safe from the outside world. The witches spend day and night strengthening and practicing their powers. Rose has the powers to either make someone tell the truth or to paralyse their body, she can also teleport. Mary is Clairevoyant, so she can hear what people think. Last of all, Edith can set fire to objects and lift up human beings without even touching them. After years of living in the coven, Rose became very self centred and big headed because she had progressed her powers a lot. She started to call herself the Queen of witches and would start to laugh at Edith and Mary because their powers were not as strong as hers. Rose eventually became the head of the coven because she was the strongest witch, Rose loved this title that she had been honoured with because it gave her control over the other witches and she could basically get her sister witches to do anything she needed. More years passed and the routine remained the same. Rose was always stronger and Mary and Edith felt less appreciated.

Chapter Eight
SHE'S A LOST CAUSE

Back to the present day: It has now been one whole day since Sister Agnes has been kidnapped. Father Elliot is in the Southbrook church sacristy preparing for evening mass. To him, everything seems normal and he is expecting Sister Agnes to show up for mass as usual. He is completely unaware of the ordeal that Sister Agnes has been and is currently going through. He kneels down to pray the rosary with his rosary beads before standing and walking to the pulpit to open up the mass. He greets all of the churchgoers but then looks out to see if everyone has attended and notices that one of the most important people from the church is missing, Sister Agnes. He gets a sinking feeling in his stomach, pauses for a second but then clears his throat and continues with mass. Father Elliot feels extremely uneasy for the whole of mass but pushes through because it is his work for the lord. However, after mass and the church is now empty, Father Elliot has some time to reflect in the chapel. He kneels down, lights a candle and asks the lord where Sister Agnes is. Suddenly he opens his eyes wide and his heart pauses for a nano second.

"Oh, my!" Gasps Father Elliot to himself. "I must go and see if she is okay" he continues. Father Elliot has now remembered the conversation he and Agnes had only just the day before. He rushes through the nave and out the big church doors, locks them and makes his way to Webber Alley where the witches live. He walks at such a fast pace and is so worried that he is gasping for air and must have a break. He stops next to a garage.

"Uh" he grunts as he tries to catch his shallow breath. He presses himself against the garage until he catches his breath. Then he starts to walk less fast as he wants to be more careful about not being caught. It is nighttime and Father Elliot is scared, so he stays very careful when he gets near to the house. He is stood at the end of the street and can see the house.

"Oh my lord. I can only imagine what they're doing to her in there" he whispers to himself. He begins walking down the street but then hears a cackle in the distance in front of him. Father Elliot begins to get breathless again and has a panic attack. He bends down to hide but also so that he can breathe better. He huffs and puffs, but tries to stay calm down so that he can go and help Sister Agnes escape. But Father Elliot's panic attack continues and he realises that it is too dangerous for him to go to the house. So, he decides that it is probably too late for Sister Agnes to be saved anyway, he concludes that she is either already dead or too weak to survive. Father Elliot decides to leave Sister Agnes in the past and just declare that she is missing at the next mass in the church. He turns around, makes the sign of the cross and says a prayer for Agnes, hoping that she will meet the lord soon and be in a better place. He turns his back to Agnes, squints his eyes to fight back tears and slowly begins to walk back to the church.

 Meanwhile, back inside the coven: Mary has gotten to the bottom of the stairs, she steps forwards to continue walking but Rose snaps her fingers and Mary is now paralysed. Edith is in the garden watering her herbs but she sees through the window what has happened to Mary and puts her watering can down. Edith cannot see Rose, however she knows that she is to blame for the paralysis of Mary so she is careful not to make a sound as she goes to enter the house. Rose continues to walk down the stairs, laughing and feeling smug because now Mary cannot do anything. She gets to the bottom of the stairs and stands in front of her. "NOW YOU CAN STAY THERE UNTIL YOU LEARN HOW TO RESPE…"

 STAB. STAB. STAB. Edith has sneaked in quietly through the backdoor and stabbed Rose in the back three times with her gardening shears. Rose screams in agony but is still conscious. Edith then sandwiches Rose's fingers between the blades of the sheers slowing cutting the skin and shouts "CLICK THESE FINGERS AND ALLOW MARY TO MOVE" into Rose's ear. Rose cannot stand the pain anymore so she slaps her fingers and Mary is released. "THERE, I RELEASED HER! NOW HELP ME SISTERS. I AM BLEEDING" panics Rose. "Help you? Ha!" laughs Edith as she chops off Rose's fingers. "OWWWWWWW" screams Rose in pain. "MY POWERS! THEY ARE USELESS NOW!

WHAT HAVE YOU DONE TO ME!" She continues to scream. "WHO IS THE ONE WITH THE USELESS POWERS NOW?" Yells Edith. "HOW DARE YOU BETRAY US LIKE THIS?" She continues. "MARY, HELP ME, NOW IS OUR CHANCE TO GET RID OF HER. THEN WE HAVE THE MOST POWERS AND IT WILL BE US WHO HAVE THE CONTROL." Mary smiles and agrees with Edith. "Let's lock her with Agnes" says Edith. "We can torture them together" replies Mary. "NO, NO, NO… you can't do this to me!" shouts Rose. "Watch us" says Mary smiling. Edith and Mary grab Rose as she cries and lift her to carry her up the stairs. They get to the third floor and unlock Agnes' door to throw her in. "THERE. You both can enjoy each other's company" laughs Edith before slamming and locking the door.

Rose has now been eliminated of her powers, humiliated in front of the rest of the coven and thrown into the room where the woman she has just been torturing is also being held captive. Rose lays on the floor, sobbing, asking why Mary and Edith would do such a thing, but deep down she knows that it is because she did not treat them well and they wanted to rebel against her.

"What on earth has happened to you?" says a calm Agnes.

"It's an outrage. Mary and Edith chopped off my fingers and took my powers away. Now to make it even worse they have thrown me into this cave with you. Oh goodness it reeks so foul in here!" Replies Rose.

"Well, dear Rose, there is only you to blame for the smell in here. But oh well, I guess now the blood running from your fingers can blend in with the smell of Edward's blood" says Agnes.

"That is so disgusting. Well, it's just a shame my blood is useless to them, since I'm not a virgin" says Rose flicking her hair over her shoulder. Agnes makes the sign of the cross. "Yes, I could get any man to play with me. I mean look at me, how could they resist the temptation. Mary and Edith are and always have been seething with jealousy. To be honest, from me to you, I don't think they have ever even been fucked. I mean just look at how hideous they look" she continues.

"PLEASE. Mind your language. Foul lady" spits Agnes in an aggressive manner.

Chapter Nine
A CUNNING PLAN

"But what will I do now? I am useless locked in here. They will torture me. I would rather die" whimpers Rose.

"Well, listen, we are both in the same ship now, aren't we? We are both being held in here, we are both going to be tortured. Why not work together to get out of here?" Agnes cunningly suggests.

"Are you out of your mind? I am not helping you to get out of here. I am the reason you're in here in the first place!" Replies Rose.

"Yes, but how else are you going to get out of being in here for the rest of your life now? Think logically. I have been betrayed by my religion, by my very own people. They haven't even cared to come and look for me. The people of the church have tremendously betrayed me" says a weak and tearful Agnes.

Rose begins to cook up a cunning plan.

"What a great idea, Agnes. Oh it would be so perfect. You have been betrayed so much by your people, you are so correct. Father Elliot and the rest of those Jesus freaks never came to save you. Oh you must be raging. How about, YOU tell me the secrets of the church and where and when we can bust into a mass and slaughter them all. This would make me look so great again in the eyes of Edith and Mary, they would let me back into the coven and I would be in power again! I can use one of the dead bodies' fingers to sew onto my stumps so that I can regain my powers! This is perfect!" Screams Rose with excitement.

"Well, what do I get out of this?" Says Agnes.

"Firstly, you get the satisfaction of knowing that the people whom have wronged you are now dead. Secondly, you can live here, join the sisterhood and rule this town with me" Replies Rose.

"Okay, the Lord will forgive me, because he loves me unconditionally. These people have wronged me and the Lord, oh how I wish for them to die!" Rages Agnes.

"Great! So, let's make arrangements. How do we get all of the church members together in order to kill them all? We can't go killing them individually as it would take too long and they would fight against us" says Rose.

"Well, it's simple. Every Sunday, the church hosts a mass for all the church goers. Oh how I miss being there and preaching the words of my lord. But we could go there then, with weapons, and kill every single one of them" replies Agnes.

"PERFECT" drools a wide eyed Rose.

"EDITH! MARY!" Rose screams.

"What are you doing?!" Shouts Agnes.

"I'm going to tell them our plan! We need all the people in this coven to work with us! They cannot keep me in here anymore. I have served our coven greatly now, they will let me back in!" Says an excited Rose. Mary and

Edith hear Rose shouting their names continuously, they look at each other, sigh and go to the staircase to go up to the third floor to Rose and Agnes' room.

"WHAT?" Bellows Edith, swinging open the door and frightening Agnes and Rose.

"GOODNESS! You scared me!" Says Agnes.

"Shut up and go to sleep old hag. What do you want Rose?" Asks Mary. Agnes seems shocked.

"Me and Agnes here have actually had a lengthy conversation about the Jesus freaks. Sisters we have a plan" expressed Rose.

"Do tell us more" says a curious Mary.

"Agnes is on our side now. She feels betrayed by the people in this town. She has given us a way to kill all the church goers. The Sunday mass, held every morning at the town Church. We must get everyone from the coven on board, we need weapons, then we can all go and attack!" Shouts Rose. Edith and Mary slowly turn to each other, lock eyes and look kind of happy, yet kind of scared. They want to use this plan because it is what they have always wanted for the coven, to kill the catholics so that they can live in peace and rule the town and make witch hunting illegal. But at the same time, they both know that they will have hell to pay from Rose after what they had done to her. So, they pretend like that is the very reason they wanted to throw her in with Agnes, because they knew that Agnes would have no other option but to confide in Rose in order to be released.

"This is exactly what we wanted. Oh Rose, of course we only threw you in here because we knew that as a result Agnes would confide in you and it would save all of us witches! Oh Rose, it is a great plan" says a stumbling Edith.

"Great. Then so be it. Release me and Agnes and we can begin to orchestrate the destruction" says Rose. Mary and Edith agree to let them free out of this room.

"Could I please be dressed now?" Asks Agnes.

"Of course" replies Mary.

"MAID!" Shouts Rose. Fiona is downstairs dusting but drops her duster to attend to Rose.

"COMING!" She shouts from the third floor. Fiona runs up the stairs and gets to the bathroom.

"Get Agnes some clothes will you?" Says Rose.

"Of course, madam" replies Fiona, whisking off to go to her maid's quarters on the third floor to get the clothing. A few minutes later she returns.

"Here are some spares, Agnes" she says, throwing them into Agnes' arms.

"Thank you, but what about my holy garments, my veil?" Questions Agnes.

"Well, there would be some trouble with that, since we burnt them on the fire" replies Edith.

"Goodness. Oh well, these will do" says Agnes, slipping on her petticoat, waistcoat and apron, the same clothing that the witches are wearing. Agnes is now dressed.

Mary and Edith both stand aside, leaving the doorway free for Rose and Agnes to walk out.

"I'M FREE! I'M FREE!" Yells an ecstatic Agnes running through the doors and down the staircase.

"GET HER! SHE IS GOING TO ESCAPE!" Shouts Rose. However, Mary and Edith reassure Rose that all the doors and windows in the house are locked and there is no way for her to escape.

"I WILL NOT ESCAPE THIS PLAN! I WANT THIS JUST AS MUCH AS ALL OF YOU NOW!" Shouts Agnes from the bottom of the stairs.

"Okay, well, then let's get everyone else to join us in the living room and we can light the fire and exchange ideas on how to execute them all" says Rose deviously.

Mary, Edith, Agnes, Rose are now all stood at the bottom of the grand staircase, joined by Fiona who heard all the commotion whilst she was cleaning in the living room.

"LADIES, LADIES! COME OUT OF YOUR ROOMS! IT IS THE TIME WE HAVE ALL BEEN WAITING SO LONG FOR" screams Rose up the stairs aimed at the third floor where the rest of the witches are living in their rooms.

All of the witches rush from their rooms to hear the good news. They stand on the staircase with their eyes gleaming with excitement.

"What is it?" questions Juliet, the trainee witch.

"The day has finally come, ladies. As most of you might know. Myself, Edith and Mary kidnapped Sister Agnes from the town church to bring her here as a pawn in order to display her to the church so that they would be threatened into banning witch hunting. However, nobody came back here to even look for Agnes, so now she is admittedly on our side. So do not be afraid of her, she has the same plans in mind as we all do for the monstrous human beings. Agnes confided in me and has told me how we can round up the people of the church in order to kill them, leaving us witches with the role of running this town. No longer will our people be executed" replies a frantically happy Rose.

"Now, ladies, follow me and come and take a seat" says Edith as she turns around and begins to walk into the living room.

"Fiona, you can go up to bed now, I'm sure Agnes can fill you in on our plans tomorrow" continues Edith. Fiona bows down to Edith and briskly walks towards and up the stairs. The witches stampede down the stairs and follow one another into the living room. Agnes, Mary, Rose and Edith take a seat next to the old wooden fireplace. The rest of the witches are seated in front of them like school children on wooden chairs.

"Pass me the matches, Agnes" says Edith. Agnes reaches down to grab them from infront of her feet on the floor. She passes them to Edith. CHHHHH. Edith forcefully strikes the match and creates the flame, then throws it into the fire place illuminating the dark room and casting shadows on the walls.

"Well that goodness for that, it is rather cold in here, i'm shivering" says Agnes.

"Shut the hell up you lord worshiping piece of ---" says one of the other witches aggressively jumping up from her chair.

"ENOUGH OF THAT! Agnes, is helping us and we need her help. Carry on with your rambling and you can be gone with the catholics!" Shouts Rose. The witch becomes silent and fearfully lowers back down to her seat.

"Infact, Edith, could you go and get us all some whiskey? To celebrate" asks Rose.

"Of course, Rose" says Edith submissively as she whisks off to get the whiskey from the kitchen. A few minutes later, Edith returns with a bottle of whiskey and some glasses.

"Well you can count me out of that, I would never dream of letting this unholy liquid tarnish my soul" huffs Agnes.

"Hm, red wine instead? The blood of christ, correct? I mean, you've seen enough blood in your stay here. Why not drink some?" laughs Rose.

SMASH. Agnes whacks a glass out of Rose's hand it shatters on the ground.

"DO NOT ASSOCIATE YOUR SATANIC RITUALS TO THE BLOOD OF MY SAVIOR YOU VIRGIN

BLOOD CRAVING VAMPIRE!" Shouts Agnes. Rose glabs a shard of the glass, gets Agnes into a head lock and holds it to Agnes' throat slowly pressing into saggy, wrinkled skin.

"DO NOT ACT OUT AROUND THESE WITCHES! THEY WILL GET RID OF YOU BEFORE YOU CAN SAY BIBLE. WE ARE ALL A TEAM NOW, AGNES. DO NOT MAKE US KILL YOU, TOO!" Screams Rose as she begins to release Agnes from the head lock.

"Now come on, let me fill up everybody's glass" says Edith unscrewing the metal cap of the whiskey bottle. She walks around the room filling all of the witches' glasses half way.

"That should be enough" she says, screwing the lid back on after circulating the room filling up the glasses. Edith gets back into her seat. Rose slurps a sip of her whiskey and says

"So, Agnes, tell everybody else what you told me" Agnes replies "Well, my people betrayed me. You brought me here and I was almost certain that the purple at the church would come to look for me. However they abandoned me. So now I want just as greatly as you all to execute them all.

Chapter Ten
THE GREAT PLAN

There is a mass every single Sunday morning at 8am in the church where all the church goers go to pray and do their worshiping. So, we can arrange to go there with whatever ammunition we need to kill them all. We will approach the church and knock on the door, Father Elliot, one of my colleagues at the church, the one who has abandoned me, will open the door as anybody is allowed into the church at any time during the mass. Then, we can all rush in and do whatever we need to do" explains Agnes.

A grin starts to grow on the face of all the witches.

"It's a shame you only thought you kidnap a Jesus freak now that more than half of our population in this town has been executed, Rose" says one of the witches.

"Don't be so ungrateful. Yes it's a little late now. But we have everything set up now and there will be no more executions for people of our kind in this town after this. Those remaining in this town will be too scared of us to try anything. Plus, we have Agnes, a sacred member of the church and second in charge of the town. So now that she is with us she can change the laws on witch hunting" replies Rose arrogantly.

"Okay, so can we all run in, grab one each and snap tie them up, then saw off their limbs?!" Asks a witch.

"Well, I was think…" Rose tries to squeeze in.

"Oh, or we could slit their throats!" Says another.

"Just calm…" Rose continues.

"ALL CHURCHGOERS ARE VIRGINS, RIGHT? WE COULD SLIT THEIR THROATS AND THEN DRINK AND BATHE IN THEIR BLOOD!" Shouts a witch at the back jumping up.

"Well, they're probably not all virgins" replies Agnes.

CRASH. Rose picks up the now empty glass bottle of whiskey and slams it down on the floor causing a silence.

"STOP" she yells.

"What about the best punishment of all? We can tie them to the seats with rope and then set them all on fire. Just like they did with witches. They tied us to trees, but tying them to the church will be better because then the church will burn down too and they will still be alive to see it happen before their very own eyes. How satisfying" plans Rose.

Everybody raises their glass in agreement, apart from Agnes who never had a sip of the whiskey.

Some time goes by, it is now 3AM and the witches are all rather tipsy. They all had three glasses filled halfway with straight whiskey. Their speech is slurred and they are ready to go to sleep. By this time, Agnes had already fallen asleep on the wooden chair next to the fire as she wasn't drinking and simply became too tired. Mary, Edith and the rest of the witches, minus Rose who stays awake longer, all decide to call it a night and sleep on the wooden floor. They are all now fast asleep. Rose gets up on her feet, gips as if she is going to be sick and stumbles over to where Agnes is sleeping. She takes her index finger, holds it up to her mouth, lubricates it with saliva and lowers it underneath her dress and begins to rub it against her labia. Her long fingernails scratch against her strawberry blonde wiry pubic hair. She continues to daze at Agnes, clutching the wooden chair that she is sleeping on to stop her from moaning too extremely in fear of awakening Agnes. She then pulls her hand from under her dress and holds it back up to her mouth, this time putting all four of her fingers into her mouth to coat them in saliva. She then digs back under her dress and rubs circular motions upon her labia until it turns rouge in colour. When the labia is loose, she penetrates herself with all four fingers and lets out an almighty moan.

"Ahhhh" moans Rose blissfully. She is having a drunken lesbian fantasy over seventy year old Sister Agnes. She grabs one of Agnes' fingers with her right hand as she continues to pleasure herself with her left. Drooling at the mouth, she begins to bring Agnes' finger towards her body. SHOCK. Agnes awakes as if somebody had hit her around the head with a baseball bat. Her body stiff and eyes wide open.

"WHAT... ON... EARTH" mumbles Agnes in a mortified tone barely opening her mouth.

"I, I, I, I am so sorry" gasps Rose.

"You wretched fool. Oh my goodness. You, young lady, are pleasuring yourself, in front of a seventy year old nun. DO YOU HAVE ANYTHING TO SAY RIGHT NOW?" Screams Agnus, blowing her stale breath into Rose's face.

"It is the alcohol. I swear Agnes. I am so tremendously apologetic. I will do anything for you to not tell my sisters" pleads Rose.

"OH IT IS SUCH A SIN! TO THINK YOU ALMOST PARTICIPATED ME INTO SUCH A SINFUL ACT MAKES ME WANT TO PUT MY HANDS AROUND YOUR NECK AND CHOKE YOU RIGHT NOW" yells Agnes.

"Agnes please, be quiet, they will awaken" continues to plead Rose.

"Go to sleep you wretched fool. Do not speak to me. May the lord cleanse you. Such a sinful act" says Agnes.

"Agnes I will go to sleep but please, you have to promise me you will not utter a word to anybody about this" cries Rose.

"I don't need to tell anybody you silly woman. I do not wish to relay this sickening act to anybody. It is pitiful. Only the lord has already seen. So you will go to hell for sure" says Agnes, still mortified.

Chapter Eleven

THE GREAT ESCAPE

Rose lays down on the floor and curls into a ball with her long ginger locks tucked under her back.

 Agnes, still sat on her chair, pretends to sleep until she can hear Rose snoring. When Rose starts to snore Agnes sets out on a mission. She spots her bible in with the rest of the books on the bookshelf in the living room, she rushes over to it and grabs it from the shelf.

 "Oh lord. I need you more than ever now. They are planning to murder OUR people! Oh lord, I cannot let this happen. Lord, please, what should I do?" Says Agnes clutching her bible with exhausted tears streaming down her face. Suddenly, a light bulb turns on in her head.

 "Ahhhh" she gasps.

 "Thank you Lord. We will all be saved" she mumbles to herself. Agnes has a plan. She puts her bible back into the bookshelf, exactly where it was, so that when the witches wake up they will have no idea anything happened during the night. She then turns around. SQUEAK. When Agnes turns, a floorboard creaks underneath her. Rose huffs and Agnes thinks that she has blown her cover. But, Rose lays still and continues to snore. Agnes takes a deep breath and carefully puts one foot in front of the other and makes her way over to where Rose is laid. She stands over Rose's body with the light of the fire still lit behind her illuminating her.

 "How on earth am I going to do this?" Whispers Agnes to herself. She sighs and does it anyway. Agnes squats down so that her arm will reach. She reaches out her still blood stained arm and slowly puts it into Rose's apron, tickling the cotton. Agnes squints her eyes in fear of being caught as she whooshes around inside Rose's apron to find the key for the house, however Agnes cannot feel it anywhere in there.

 "Good lord" whimpers Agnes as she begins to walk over to Mary who might have the key in her apron. Agnes follows the same process. CLINK. Agnes' long dirty nails touch the large metal key.

Agnes feels so liberated that she lets out a tiny screech but then runs back to pretend she is sleeping on her chair when she hears one of the other witches moving. She sits there with the key in between her thighs, with her head nodded and snoring. The witch whom was moving, stands up and walks out of the room. Agnes squints her eyes to see who it is and it is a short and large lady with tanned skin. The witch turns the corner and so Agnes remains still and snoring. A minute later the witch returns to the living room sipping a glass of water, she then lays back down. Agnes waits a good twenty minutes just to make sure that the witch has fallen asleep again. Then she makes her move. She stands up from her chair and hops out of the living room trying to avoid creaking the floor boards. Now all Agnes has to do is walk down the corridor and through the hallway and she will be able to get out. She walks at a fast pace through the corridor breathing heavily, so far so good, then she runs through the hallway and gets to the grand front door. This door is huge and has a huge pentagram statue stuck onto it. Agnes gulps and pulls out the key from her apron. She slots the key into the door lock, carefully trying to not make any noise and then turns the key one hundred and eighty degrees until she hears a click. CLICK. The grand door is now open, Agnes is so close to freedom. She slowly pulls open the door, with both hands as it is so heavy. She sees the greenery and nature outside and falls to her knees exhaustedly.

"Oh lord. I can finally see your beautiful work again. I can feel your oxygen and see your trees. Oh what a delight" whimpers Agnes with tears dripping into her mouth.

"But there is no time for this, I just get to Father Elliot quickly and arrange our own set of plans that these satanists would never expect in a million years. Oh they will be so blind sighted. Poor, poor, witches. Soon they will be the ones who are saying bye bye to the world. How stupid they are to think that I would ACTUALLY help them" cackles Agnes to herself as she steps outside onto the doorstep and closes the door behind her. She leaves it unlocked so that she can get back inside without making much noise. Agnes is now outside, it is five o'clock in the morning and the weather is stormy. A gust of crisp wind blows through her free uncovered hair as she smiles and sniffs up the scent of nature. She begins to skip down from the house, barefooted with gravel getting wedged in between her toes, to get onto the street. After she has completely left the premises of the witches' coven, she skips down Webber Alley and turns the corner onto Bettor Drive, she follows the road and turns left but it only leads her to a cul-de-sac.

"Hmm" grunts Agnes, seemingly lost. She is trying to look for the Parish where Father Elliot will be sleeping. She goes turns around and goes back to the top of Bettor Drive and this time turns right, leading onto a Sandstone Avenue, this road does not lead to a dead end for as far as Agnes can see, so she follows the road. Huffing and puffing, Agnes walks until she gets to the end of the road, but the Parish is still not in sight. Agnes then turns the corner onto Outwhere Yard where there is a graveyard filled with tombstones. Agnes decides that she will walk through the graveyard in order to get to the back of the streets. Agnes walks one hundred and eighty degrees in a circle around the graveyard to get to the entrance. In the darkness, Agnes sees a flock of crows walking upon the land of the graveyard.

"My goodness!" says Agnes as she quickly makes the sign of the cross and squints her eyes. Agnes knows that seeing crows in a graveyard is a superstition for bad look. Regardless, she continues and walks to the entrance of the graveyard. Finally, agnes gets to the entrance. She pulls open the wooden gate. SQUEAK. The hinges of the gate squeak piercingly loudly.

"GOOD HEAVENS!" Whispers Agnes to herself. The high pitch squeak scares the crows in the graveyard and they start squawking and flap away above the treetops. Luckily there are not many houses on Outwood Yard, so it is likely that nobody heard the loud squeak of the gate or the squawking of the crows. Agnes once again huffs in despair and walks through the gate, being careful when she closes it so that it won't squeak again so loudly. Crunch. Snap. Pop. There are fallen twigs on the ground of the graveyard which Agnes is tiptoeing on.

"OUCH!" She gently shouts. One of the twigs has snapped under her toes and stabbed into her little toe. She lifts her foot up and it appears to be bleeding. Agnes needs something to tie around the cut to stop the bleeding and prevent infection. So, she tears away a strip of the material from her white apron with her long, dirty fingernails and bandages it around her toe. Agnes, now hobbling quietly, is being careful not to wake anybody else up in fear that they would ruin her plan. She only wishes to speak to Father Elliot. She tiptoes through all of the fallen leaves, twigs and branches from the entrance of the graveyard to the exit of the graveyard. Agnes opens the same looking wooden gate slowly to reduce the volume of a potential squeak, but luckily there is no squeak from this gate. Agnes walks out of the churchyard and turns the corner onto Downtree Boulevard, stops to have a look down the street and all of a sudden she sees the large, sacred building.

"Finally!" whispers Agnes to herself with glee, as she begins to walk down the street to the large, sanctified doors of the Parish where Father Elliot will surely be deep into his sleep. Gasping with exhaustion from all the walking and tip toeing, Agnes has finally made it onto the premises of the Parish.

"Oh some holiness" cries Agnes as she bends down on the doorstep of the Parish to pray.

"Dear Lord, my saviour. I know now that all of this was your good work. You knew that it would be the only way to get rid of these witches once and for all! I will be forever grateful that you chose me, to serve you in such a humongous task. I will not let you down. Lord, I ask you to protect me, just a little bit more for these next couple of days, then I will have my freedom" prays an emotional Agnes. Mid way through her praying, hailstones start to quickly descend from the sky.

"Lord, I know it is you!" Squeeks Agnes with a wide smile on her face as the stones of ice pitter - patter off of her body and onto the ground. She stays kneeled down with her hands reached out either side of her body and her chin raised up towards the early morning dark skies. She stays in this position of worship for a few minutes before levelling back onto her feet and brushing the fresh hailstones away from her already soaking clothes. She takes a couple of deep breaths and then raises her left hand.

Knock. Knock. Knock.

Agnes lifts the wet metal door knocker with her bony, wrinkled fingers and knocks three times being careful to not be too loud, but just loud enough for Father Elliot to wake. She stands in front of the large wooden door with her hands tightly intertwined, hailstones still falling, anticipating Father Elliot parting the doors. She patiently waits outside for two minutes, with each minute feeling like a week, with her teeth grinding together tightly. She cups her ear with her hand and presses against the door to listen if she can hear Father Elliot coming to the door. She hears Father Elliot snoring quietly and breathing heavily, but not getting up to answer the door. Agnes gulps her saliva with anxiety, knowing that she is running out of time to get back to the Coven before the witches begin to wake. She raises her hand once more. Knock. Knock. Knock. Knock.

Agnes knocks a further four times. Once again, she places her ear against her cupped hand on the wooden door. STOMP. The snoring stops and Agnes hears a stomp on the ground from inside the Parish. Agnes knocks once more just in case the knocks had woken him up but he hadn't consciously heard them. STOMP. STOMP. STOMP. Agnes, without her ear even being against the door, hears more and more stomping. Agnes stands in front of the door anticipating Father Elliot opening it. SQUEAK. A sleepy Father Elliot pulls open the heavy wooden door. Father Elliot and Agnes, at long last, are reunited.

Chapter Twelve
A CHANGE OF HEART

"Can I help you?" Asks Father Elliot squinting and rubbing his eyes.

"FATHER ELLIOT!" Screams Agnes as she drops to her knees and lets out an almighty cry.

"GOODNESS GRACIOUS! SISTER AGNES, IS THAT YOU?!" Shouts a suddenly very awake and wide eyed Father Elliot.

"IT IS ME!" Replies Agnes.

"LORD ABOVE! I could hardly recognise you without your veil! Sister Agnes I am so glad that our Lord showed you the way home. I did come and loo" Father Elliot gets cut off by Agnes.

"Listen. There is no time for talking. Just listen"
She expresses.

"But Agnes I just want to make sure you know that I" Father Elliot tries to squeeze in.

"LISTEN! The witches! They are still in the same house and they have tortured me endlessly. They stripped me of my holy garments and bible and made me bathe in Edward's blood!" She shouts.

"Edward. Edward the alter boy who had gone missing?" Questions Father Elliot.

"YES! It was all their doing. They made me eat him too! But enough of this. I came here to tell you the plan and then I must go! The witches think that I am going to bring them to the church during Sunday morning mass to annihilate the people of the church. Really I just want to lure them here so we can kill them all instead! So we will be at the church doors on Sunday and you must all be prepared. Father Elliot we need salt, a lot of it. To cover all of them and stop them from using their powers. Then you must all grab them and we will burn them all when they are tied to the trees. Mass must not go ahead. You must all instead hide in the chapel, I will bring the witches inside and say that mass is due to start and then you will carry out the attack. Father Elliot I trust you and the Lord enough to know that this plan will be carried out immaculately and these witches will be no more!" Says a pleading and anxious Agnes.

"Agnes! I just cannot believe any of this!" Says Father Elliot.

"Well, believe it and start preparing tomorrow for the witches' arrival. We must succeed in killing them all" says Agnes.

"Now I must go. I shall see you very soon Father Elliot. I will pray for you" she continues before running away from the Parish on her way back to the coven before the witches awake and realise that she has escaped.

"AGNES WAIT! I NEED TO TELL YOU!" Screams Father Elliot as Agnes runs away.

Agnes does not stop and just continues to run until she is no longer in Father Elliot's sight. Father Elliot gasps, before stepping back inside the Parish and closing the doors. He sits on his mattress in the pitch black darkness, with shock illuminating his eyes.

"My oh my. Sister Agnes. We have a lot of work to do" he whispers to himself, slowly lowering his body back down to the mattress. Father Elliot lays stiff for quite some time before eventually drifting off again.

Meanwhile, Agnes is now running through the streets of Southbrook like a raving lunatic trying to get back inside the coven before sunrise and the arising of the witches. Agnes has fastly made her way back to the graveyard, she opens the wooden gate again being careful not to make any loud noises. Once she gets through the gate she continues to run on the unsteady and now wet, muddy ground. SLAM. Agnes slams her stomach into the corner of a headstone in the graveyard and drops bends to her knees whilst squinting and hissing in agony.

"YYYY-OUCH" muffles Agnes. She is in pain but she must continue. She gets back onto her feet and continues to run. Seventy year old Sister Agnes is now running barefoot with a wounded toe and a winded stomach. She makes her way through to the other side of the graveyard and reaches for the gate, remembering the loud sound it had made on her arrival, so she once more opens it very slowly. Now that Agnes is out of the graveyard, all she has to do is run down a few streets and then get back to the coven. Agnes goes back down Sandstone Avenue and finds a little, dark and narrow alleyway. Agnes follows the alleyway and low and behold it leads straight to the top of Webber Alley. Agnes is so close to returning to the coven without being caught by the witches.

"Ha! I did it! Oh lord, thank you for the guidance" pants Agnes and she sets off running again. Running on the pathway against the gust with leaves blowing in her face, Agnes gets to the Coven. There is no light shining from the house, so Agnes is sure that nobody is awake inside.

"Phew!" Agnes blows from her lips. She steps into the front garden and makes her way to the large and spooky looking door. Smiling and cackling with a feeling of achievement, she dips both of her scrawny hands into her apron to retrieve the large metal key. Suddenly, her heart plunges to her stomach like a faulty elevator plummeting and crashing to the ground floor at one thousand miles per hour, or an aeroplane losing power to all four of its engines and nose diving into the Pacific Ocean. The key is missing.

"AGNES! FOOL!" She shouts to herself with her body trembling and eyes bulged. Suddenly she raises her hand and grabs her mouth, reminding her not to shout, or even breathe loudly, as she is directly in front of the entry to the house. She lifts up her apron to look for the key in case she has missed it with her hand, only to discover that it was because she had ripped the material from her apron to bandage her toe, so there was now a hole. She throws her apron back down and swiftly swings her body around. With her back now to the entrance she whispers to herself "Holy fool! How careless of you!" She sets off again, leaving the house, now on a mission to find the key. She turns back onto Webber Alley, facing down and scanning all crevasses of the pathway as she is walking. Her eyes swinging from left to right and right to left, she picks up the pace and starts to fast walk, with her eyes starting to become moist from the wind.

A tear forms and swims down her left cheek, she sniffles and wipes her eyes and continues to search.

"Lord help me, I am running short of time" Agnes prays to herself under her breath as she wanders down the street. She has wandered the entire street of Webber Alley and found absolutely nothing. She huffs and turns once again onto Bettor Drive and follows the same process. Out of the corner of her damp eye she sees a glistening on the top of a puddle further down the street but convinced herself it is more than likely just the moonlight shining onto the water causing the glistening texture. But as she continues to get closer to this puddle she realises that it is strange how only a part of the puddle is now glistening. She grunts and stops searching the street to just go straight to this puddle and investigate. Agnes stands over the puddle, sees her old reflection in the water… along with the large metal key sunken at the bottom. A tear, this time not from the wind, but from relief, drops into the puddle. Agnes stands, resting for a few moments to catch her breath, before lowering herself and dipping her hand into the murky puddle caused by the hailstones. She pulls out the key and wipes it with the underneath of her petticoat to dry and clean it. She then turns back around, splashing her feet in the puddle and begins to go back to the house. Agnes runs down Bettor Drive and turns back onto Webber Alley, finally, she is back at the house. Agnes has made it, just before sunrise. It is now six o'clock in the morning and Agnes is pressed up against the door of the coven, absolutely destroyed and exhausted from the nights' events. She lays against it, with her toe bloody, the soles of her feet muddy and her clothes soaking. Agnes realises that she must clean herself up before the witches awake, otherwise surely they would be aware of the fact Agnes has been up to no good. It is time for Agnes to finally enter back into the house. She once more, pulls her hand into her apron, her nails clink against the key as Agnes sighs with comfort and relief, she then pulls the key to the lock as if she is holding a gun, inserts the key and twists it one hundred and eighty degrees until she hears a… CLICK. The door is now unlocked. Agnes makes the sign of the cross three times with her eyes closed, hoping and praying inside her head that nobody awake is on the other side of the door.

 "Lord, I have served good work tonight. I have saved our people. Please just let me overcome this last hurdle" Agnes fastly prays to herself. She pushes the door, very timidly, until there is a slight view from the outside. Agnes pushes her face up against the side of the door where the view is clear and looks to see if she can see anybody awake. But, pleasantly for Agnes, she is greeted only by great snores.

"Perfect" she whispers to herself. Agnes then opens the door just wide enough for her to be able to squeeze her skinny body through. She enters. Inside the coven it is still very very dark, so, Agnes grabs a candle from a pile of tea lights on the floor which the witches would use if they needed some light to guide them around the house if they woke up in the middle of the night. STRIKE. Agnes strikes a match and lights the small candle. She closes the door carefully and locks it behind her. Firstly, she walks along the long hallway, with no problems, then we gets to the corridor where the room is in which the witches are sleeping. CREAK. The floorboard creaks. Agnes shuts her eyes and prays that it was not loud enough for any of the witches to hear it. She then gets to the living room where the witches are sleeping, which is still illuminated by the fire. Agnes rests her candle on the floor and stands in the doorway, casting a shadow of herself onto the wall, staring at all of the witches' bodies. Nobody has moved a muscle. Agnes is safe. She is now less worried about being caught and starts to relax some more. She very gently enters the room. She tiptoes past Rose.

"Filthy fool" she mutters. Then she goes to Edith to return the key. Agnes takes out the key from her apron and reaches back inside Edith's apron and drops the key inside. Now that the key has been returned and the house looks untouched, Agnes needs to look the same. She must change her clothes and clean herself, so that it is evident she has not been anywhere, but simply sleeping. She picks her candle up from the floor and exits the warm, fire lit room and hobbles her way to the grand staircase, this time remembering where the creaking floorboard is and avoiding it like the plague. She tightly squints her eyes, grits her teeth and then raises her left, muddy foot to take her first step onto the grand wooden staircase. To Agnes' relief, there is silence, the staircase made no creaking noises, she must now climb sixty more steps to get to the third floor where the maid's quarters are. Agnes slowly climbs the first twenty steps of the grand staircase until she reaches the first floor. She gets over the nineteenth step, puts her candle down and collapses to the floor in exhaustion. Seventy year old Agnes has been on the run all night and it has taken a toll on her body, but she knows that she is so close to completing her mission and she has faith in her lord that she will pull through, so she crawls back up from the floor and continues on to the next twenty steps. She gets to the second floor and this time does not fall, she continues all the way to the third floor. Now, witch her candle guiding her down the corridor, Agnes huffs and gasps and hobbles her way to Fiona's maid's quarters to get some clean clothes. She walks into the room and sees

Fiona laid there, on her mattress on the floor, fast asleep. She walks over to where Fiona is laid.

"Fiona!" She whispers as she taps her head with her index finger. Fiona does not wake up. Agnes then winds a bunch of Fiona's hair around her index finger and yanks it.

"OUCH!!" Yells Fiona, suddenly waking up.

"SHUSH!" Spits Agnes.

"You must be quiet!" She continues.

"Why on earth did you do that?" Asks Fiona, rubbing her scalp.

"Because firstly, I need some help getting cleaned up and" says Agnes.

"WAIT. What happened to you? Why are you so mucky? Did you all decide to take the house party, or coven party should I say, into the garden? The neighbors won't be happy about that!" Interrupts Fiona.

"SHUUUUSH! I need to tell you. There was no party in any garden. I escaped" says Agnes. Fiona gasps harshly.

"GOOD HEAVENS! Agnes that is awfully risky! You risked your whole life! But how did you pull that off without anybody finding out?" Asks Fiona.

"Well, they all fell asleep in the living room, quite careless if you think about it, the key to unlock the grand entrance was inside Edith's apron!" Explains Agnes.

"Ha! Isn't it just fabulous how I have been trapped here for two whole years and every single night they lock that key in a secret place that still to this day I cannot find.

Then magically they have a few drinks and become incapable of anything" laughs Fiona.

"Well, maybe you won't make it to a third year being stuck in here. I have everything planned out. I must allow you to be on my side, as a fellow catholic" says Agnes.

"Good Lord, Agnes! You have been up to no good, but I like the sound of this! Do continue!" Says Fiona jumping up out of bed and standing infront of Agnes with a huge grin upon her face.

"Well, here it goes. I got the key, got out of the door and collapsed to the ground because for the first time in nearly a week I could smell our lord's creation once more. The smell of the trees and grass was quite extraordinary" says Agnes. Fiona sheds a tear and then starts to sob.

"I need to get out of this place. I have a family. I miss them so much" says Fiona. Agnes reaches out her finger and wipes away Fiona's tears, smiling.

"Dear, we will get out of here. Our faith should be stronger now than ever. We must pray to our lord that my plan works though" says Agnes.

"Okay, I'm fine, please continue" says Fiona, sniffling up her tears.

"Okay. So, I exited the house. Then very carefully made my way through the graveyard, which explains why I am so disgustingly muddy, to get to the Parish where Father Elliot sleeps and spends his free time. I knocked on the door, only to hear him continuing to snore, so I knocked again and a little bit louder. Then I could hear him through the wall walking towards the door. I have never felt so free and relieved. I could finally talk to him and tell him everything that has happened to me and about this whole place. I had to be quick because I needed to get back here before sunrise. So I just told him that on Sunday, he should expect all of us turning up at the church to kill all of the church people, so that he can prepare to actually, kill the witches instead. We will be fine, obviously, for we are not witches, so you needn't worry about that. But he is going to create a plan in order to kill all of them, then we will all be safe. So now, we keep it a secret and pretend to be on the same side as the witches, but little do they know what fate awaits them" cackles Agnes.

"OH, AGNES! What a great, great idea! How on earth did you get so brave? I am always so terrified in this place and would not dream of trying to escape. We must be careful, if they know about this, they will more than likely kill you and maybe even me too because they could think I had some association with it" says Fiona.

"Of course, it is between us only" says Agnes with an evil grin on her face.

"Good lord Agnes, I remember from talking to Rose earlier today about the food shopping, it is Saturday just tomorrow, that gives us one more day until the carnage!" Gasps Fiona.

"Well then, let the games begin" cackles Agnes.

"Now, could you please help me clean myself up? I need to be immaculate so they cannot tell that anything is different" expresses Agnes.

"Of course, the fresh garments are right over here" says Fiona, walking to the corner of the room and blowing a cobweb from the pile of folded clothes.

Agnes slips into a fresh petticoat and then layers up with a waistcoat and apron. She decides that she should simply just burn her dirty and now damp clothes on the fireplace where the witches are sleeping to dispose of the evidence. But before she goes to do that, she wanders over to a wooden bucket of water kept in the room which Fiona uses to clean the clothes if there is a stain. Agnes bends down to her feet and unties the piece of material from her toe and adds it to the pile of material that she will burn. Her toe is covered with plum red dry blood and gravel. Agnes dips her hands into the bucket and scoops up some of the freezing cold water and splashes it onto her feet.

"PHHHHH" screeches Agnes under her breath. The freezing cold water hit the open wound on her toe and stung her.

"Goodness, Agnes, what on Earth happened now?" Asks Fiona.

"Ouch, the freezing cold water hurt the slit in my toe" replies Agnes. After the first splash, the pain is not too bad, so she continues to wash away the blood and dirt from her feet and furthermore washes the dirt from her hands too. She then uses her old petticoat to dry her feet and hands. Agnes is now fully dressed, spruced up and ready to go back downstairs to burn her pile of dirty clothes. She tells Fiona to just stay upstairs and to act like nothing ever happened. She then reaches out to grab her tea light so that she can see clearly to get back downstairs.

"OUCH" she yells, dropping the lit candle to the floor. The candle has completely melted and the metal surrounding the wax has burnt Agnes' fingers. PUFF, PUFF, PUFF. She blows out the candle on the floor quickly before any fire could break out. Luckily there was no fire, but now there is a puddle of solidified candle wax splodged on the wooden floor.

"Oh my!" Gasps Agnes.

"Don't worry, here's another one, go and sort out the old clothes. I can clean this up on the morning" says Fiona, patting Agnes on the back and handing her a new candle.

"Thank you, Fiona, good night" says Agnes, lighting the candle.

"Good night" replies Fiona. Agnes turns, smiles to Fiona and then closes the door before turning around and beginning to walk back along the corridor. Agnes, guided by her new candle, slowly walks along the corridor and then down the three flights of stairs back to the first floor. The witches are still sleeping, so Agnes uses the opportunity to burn all of her old clothes.

 She steps into the living room, the candle in one hand and her old clothes in the other. She blows out her candle as the living room is still lit by the fire and just puts it into the bin. Then, she hobbles over to the fireplace, stares into the fluorescent yellow and orange flames and smiles a big smile of achievement.

She prays "Lord, I have saved our people. I have been serving the church nearly all my life for a moment like this, I was just waiting for it. I would have never imagined being in my current situation but I guess that in hindsight I can only been thankful for being put into this position to wipe out the remaining witches in this town and save the people of the church. Thank you Lord. Amen." She then chucks the pile of clothes out of her arm into the fire and listens to the material blacken and burn into a pile of ash until the evidence is disposed of. Finally, Agnes has covered up all of her tracks. She is now exhausted so she walks a few more steps and is finally seated.

 "Ahhhh" she quietly gasps with relief as she lowers herself down to the seat. She smiles and then closes her eyes with full security knowing that her plan is now in place. Agnes relives the whole night inside her head, feeling ever so proud of herself, before then finally drifting off. Her head nods, her mouth opens and her body and mind can now rest for a few hours. When the sun comes up and the witches awake, it is time for all of these plans to be put into action.

Chapter Thirteen
BACK TO REALITY

DING. DING. DING. The large wooden grandfather clock strikes nine o'clock and begins to chime loudly. The clock is right next to the fire place where Agnes was sleeping.

"GOODNESS!" She screams.

"What is that awful sound?" She shouts covering her ears. Rose, Edith, Mary and all of the other witches awake too. They lay yawning.

"It is the grandfather clock, it's nine o'clock, time for us to wake up. We always wake up at this time" says Rose.

"How do I turn this thing off?" Shouts Agnes standing in front of the clock.

"It sounds for a whole minute, you will just have to wait" says Rose. Agnes huffs, once again covers her ears and just sits back into her chair until the noise stops. After one minute, the chiming has stopped.

"Well, thank goodness for that!" Shouts Agnes with relief.

"It is only the same as your god damned church bells interrupting us every afternoon!" Replies Edith, spitting in Agnes' face. Agnes holds her nose so she won't have to inhale Edith's morning breath exiting her crusty mouth.

"Come on, ladies, breakfast time. Today is the day. We must prepare for tomorrow" says Rose, smiling and cracking her neck from side to side.

"If it is more human flesh, then no thank you, you can count me out" says Agnes.

"No flesh for breakfast, but plenty of flesh for us after tomorrow ladies, we will be looking and feeling so youthful with all of their virgin blood" expresses Rose.

"Well, you can all enjoy, anyway, what is for breakfast?" Asks Agnes.

"Well, we should get Fiona to make us all something very special" suggests Mary.

"Great idea, Mary, I will go and get her and she can prepare it for us. For now, you can all stay in here and talk amongst yourselves, I will go and get Fiona from upstairs" says Rose, frolicking out of the room and up the stairs to the maid's quarters.

KNOCK. KNOCK. KNOCK.

"Are you decent?" Asks Rose.

"Yes" Shouts Fiona, sounding like she has just woken up from the knocks. Rose turns the door non ninety degrees and pushes open the door. She takes one foot step and then stands in the solidified melted candle wax.

"What on earth happened here? Why is there a pool of wax underneath my feet!" Asks Rose.

"Oh, I was praying last night, then I accidentally knocked off the candle from the windowsill, I'm so sorry Rose, I will get it cleaned up in no time" says Fiona.

"HA! Praying. Praying for what? You do know, that all of the people of the church in this town are going to be fresh meat tomorrow, don't you? That's right. We stayed up late last night thinking of how to kill them all, we decided it is best if we enter the church, I can paralyse them all with my power, then you and everybody else in this coven can grab one or more person and bring them outside. Whilst they are paralysed, of course they can still feel everything, so we will slit their throats and myself, Edith and Mary and the rest of the witches will all drink the blood there and then so it is as fresh as possible, then, before they die, to add some more torture, we are going to bob their heads one by one into a bucket of iced water and drown them. Then we will place all of the bodies in a pile and have to drag them all back into the coven one by one to take the best pieces of meat off of their bodies and then dispose of the rest of them and leave the bones out for the wild cats" explains Rose.

"Well, that sounds… BLAH" Fiona is sick right in front of Rose, with the spew splattering onto her feet.

"FILTHY FOOL! HOW DARE YOU!" Bellows Rose.

"Madam, I am ever so sorry, I will clean it up right now" whimpers Fiona, with sick still dribbling from her face. BANG. Rose knocks over the barrel of water to splash onto her feet to clean them.

"NOW!" Screams Rose.

"Of course, I will just get a cloth" says Fiona, turning her back to Rose to go and get a cloth. Rose screams and yanks Fiona's hair from behind and pulls her close to her body, then gets her in a headlock.

"Forget the cloth, fool, clean my feet NOW!" Screams Rose with her face red and teeth gritted together.

"Of course, madam" says a petrified Fiona dropping to the floor to clean Rose's feet. Fiona wipes away her own vomit from Rose's bare feet with the water and then dries them with her own apron.

"Thank you. Now, we have a celebratory breakfast to prepare. Come down to the kitchen with me so we can prepare it for everyone" says Rose calmly.

"Of course madam, anything that you need!" Says Fiona, standing up and brushing herself off. She follows Rose out of the room, shaking from the fright of her shouting and closes her door. Rose goes down the stairs, with her wavy strawberry - blonde locks flowing and her petticoat whooshing against the air as she briskly walks down down all three flights with Fiona following right behind her.

They both enter the kitchen.

"Okay, grab me twelve white bread rolls, the rest of the chicken and twelve apples" says Rose to Fiona.

"Of course" says Fiona skipping towards the old store room in the kitchen, almost drooling because this would be the best meal that she had ever eaten whilst being held hostage at the coven. She grabs the bread, which was baked freshly a few days prior in the Southbrook farmhouse, the apples, the half of a chicken and puts it all on the wooden kitchen table for Rose to prepare. Rose takes off her normal apron and instead puts on one hanging from the kitchen door which she wears specifically for when she could get messy in the kitchen. She pulls out a bread knife and her butchers knife from the knife block. Firstly, she inserts her butchers knife into the poultry and carves the whole half of a chicken into thin slices. Secondly, she takes her bread knife and slices all of the bread rolls down the middle. Lastly, she lays two slices of the chicken onto all of the bread rolls and puts them onto her best crockery and places the plates in front of each of the fourteen seats around the table alongside a red apple, for the twelve witches, Agnes and Fiona. Fiona boils some water and makes some tea with milk for everybody and places the tea filled mugs alongside the breakfast.

"LADIES! Breakfast is ready!" Shouts Rose. The witches and Agnes all make their way through to the kitchen.

"Take a seat and enjoy" says Fiona.

"Well, yes, but you have the cleaning up to do now Fiona, so we shall set your plate aside for now" replies Rose. Fiona's eyes turn sad.

"Of course, madam" she obeys whilst dragging herself over to the sink to wash the knives and clean the work surface where the food had been prepared. Everybody else takes a seat and tucks into their celebratory breakfast.

Chapter Fourteen
CHURCH PREPARATIONS

Meanwhile, over at the Southbrook town church, Father Elliot is breaking the plans to all of the church goers. Every catholic in the small town has attended the church, Father Elliot asks them all to take a seat in the nave whilst he goes up to the pulpit to break the news. Everybody is seated.

"Thank you everybody for joining me for mass today, however, we will actually be doing something just slightly different. As you all know, Sister Agnes has been missing for over a couple of days now, well, I have seen her. She came to the Parish to wake me in the early hours of this morning to relay some awful news. She was abducted by Rose Cartwright, one of the witches living on Webber Alley and taken to her house, which has now been converted into a safe haven for all of the remaining witches in this city. They have tortured her tremendously, she looks so awfully frail. But to get to the point, the witches have been led to believe that Agnes is on their side, however she is only pretending to be so, so that she can lure them to the church where we can then place an attack on them instead. So, today is all about planning and organising. We MUST kill these witches once and for all. So, does anybody have any suggestions on the best way to go about this?" Says Father Elliot to his audience. The audience sit stunned as if the blood and oxygen had completely drained from their bodies and they were just empty shells.

 "S-s-s-salt… we need a lot of salt, to e-e-eliminate their powers" stutters one churchgoer.

 "Yes! We could get as much salt as we possibly can, empty the shelves of every shop, then somehow make a contraption where we can hold the salt up to the ceiling and release it when the witches enter, allowing it to rain and dance all over their bodies and their powers will be turned off immediately!" Says another.

 "But we need only the purest large grain rock salt. Any old ordinary table salt simply is not strong enough" explains Father Elliot.

 "Well, I know a place, it's in nickleded, one of us could travel there. It's a little seaside only a couple of hours away! Me, my wife and our two little girls go there almost every summer for a few days. This place is famous for its pure sea salt" says another churchgoer.

 "Then so be it, you must go right now, we only have today to prepare" says Father Elliot. The man nods his head in agreement and walks out of the church, jumps into his gig and begins to make his way to nickleded. Meanwhile the rest of the people in the church start to stitch together some pieces of fabric to somehow fix to the roof of the church, attached to a string which when pulled will pull down the fabric releasing all of the salt onto the witches.

Back inside the coven, the witches, Agnes and Fiona have all just finished their celebratory breakfast. All of the witches and Agnes stand up and make their way back into the living room. Fiona collects up all of the dirty plates and stays in the kitchen to wash them up.

"Okay ladies, now who is ready for their weekly dosage of young virgin blood?" Asks Rose.

"ME! ME! ME!" Say all of the witches in unison with smiles on their face. Agnes' stomach turns and the colour of her skin drains from a slightly blushed colour to a completer corpse complexion.

"Must I stay here for that?" Questions Agnes, holding her stomach as it churns.

"Well, you have nowhere else to be, right?" Replies Rose.

"No, I guess not" says Agnes, slowly and unsurely.

"Great. Well then, I will go and get the blood. This week's blood is from a young catholic eleven year old girl, poor girl wasn't fast enough to get away. At least the running circulated all of that fresh blood for us" says Rose before she wanders out of the room to go upstairs. She goes up to the bathroom where Edward's body has now been disposed of, instead lays the body of the eleven year old girl on a bed of ice. Rose takes a butchers knife from the windowsill in the bathroom, gets onto her knees so that she is level with the body and begins to slice into the flesh, removing the most tender parts to save for a meal or two, but most importantly catching the blood in a large glass vase ready for her and the other witches to drink up in order to keep them looking and feeling rejuvenated and youthful. She puts the lumps of lean flesh back onto the ice, wipes her hands clean with the underneath of her petticoat, grabs the vase filled with thin red blood and takes it down the stairs. Rose enters the living room holding the vase with a smile on her face. The witches spring up from their seats almost with their tongues hanging out of their mouths salivating for the blood like dogs for water on a sunny day.

"Now, now. One by one we all take five sips and then pass the vase along. I will start" says Rose. She lifts the vase to her face, bows her head and sniffs the blood.

"Ahhhh" she says out loud. "It smells so young" she continues before forcefully sticking her lips onto the side of the glass vase and then tipping her head upwards to take five large sips. She bows her head back down and removes the vase from her lips. She takes the back of her hand and wipes away the excess blood drooling from around her mouth.

"Agnes, would you care to try? It would make you look and feel so much better" says Rose. Agnes looks into her eyes, then turns her head and gulps.

"No, no I am quite fine thank you. Maybe another cup of tea later if I may, but no blood for me" she says.

"Sure. Well then, Edith, your turn" says Rose, passing the large vase to her. Edith takes her five sips and then passes it on to Mary, Mary then passes it to the next witch and they go around in a circle until everybody has had five sips. The vase circulates the witches and gets back to Rose, however there is still some blood left. Rose simply just dips her hands into the bottom of the vase, scoops out as much blood as possible and then smears it onto her face and décolletage like it is a face mask.

"Mmmm" she moans almost sexually, before putting the vase down.

"Now, let's lay down the plans" she says.

"Okay, so I think that we should arrive with a lot of Rope, we can all run in and grab them. I doubt there are any weapons held in a church so they will have nothing to defend themselves, I'm sure. We can all grab as many people as possible, tie them to the trees and then I can snap my fingers and enter them into a blaze, just like they have done with the rest of our people" says Edith.

"Well, that sounds good to me" says Mary.

"That should do it. Oh my, how satisfying it will all be. To finally rid this town of the Jesus freaks" adds Rose. Agnes pouts her lips tightly to combat the urge of smiling, as she knows all too well how things are really going to plan out. Fiona, still in the kitchen, overhears the witches and smiles freely, also knowing that it will in fact be the witches who will meet their end.

"Okay, well then now, witches you make go back to your rooms and do whatever you please. Agnes, as a guest, you are more than welcome to just hang around wherever you please, explore this building, it has a lot of secrets" says Rose. The witches stand up and make their way to their rooms.

Chapter Fifteen
A BLOOD - CURDLING ART EXHIBITION

Agnes decides to explore the house. She goes through
the kitchen and through the window she sees the vibrant
green garden popping with variations of reds, pinks and
yellows from all of the different beautiful plants, also all
of the herbs planted by Edith such as rosemary, sage and
time that are spiralling around sticks of bamboo against
the walls of the wooden fence in the garden. She stares
into the garden, day dreaming that she is running around
the garden freely, picking the herbs from the walls and
sniffing them, picking the flowers and holding them in a
bunch, but then she snaps out of the day dream and the
harsh reality returns to her mind, her wide smile turns to
a poker face with no emotions, just numbness. She tries
her luck of getting into the garden by walking over to the
garden door and turning the doorknob, but of course it is
locked. Sister Agnes decides to continue strolling
around, she checks the pantry, dusting away the cobwebs
with her apron as she enters, then finds some more bread
rolls. Her stomach growls harshly, Agnes is starving, so
she decides to impulsively take a bite, not caring if she
got into trouble, however she quickly regrets it when she
learns that the bread is completely stale by chewing the
cardboard - like texture in her mouth. She spits out the
now mushed up and chewed bread into her hand, exits
the pantry and goes to throw it in the bin, she then rinses

her hands off with some cold water at the sink and pats them dry on her petticoat. She then decides to explore through more doors that she has never been able to see before, she walks around like she is in a museum. There is a door on the opposite side of the kitchen where the garden door is, with a padlock open hanging from it, Agnes ceases the opportunity to go through and see what is behind. As she enters it is dark, again she is greeted by cobwebs. She whooshes them away with her hands and this time as she fastly pulls her hand through the thick cobwebs she feels a very large, thick bodied spider fall into her palm. Agnes squeals and throws her hand down towards the floor and the spider scatters away. She decides to step back out of the room to get a candle so that she can see where she is going. She grabs a pre burned candle from the kitchen side and a pack of matches. She slides open the box, takes out a match and strikes harshly until the flame sizzles, she then holds it down onto the candle wick until it is lit, she then puts the matches down, picks up her candle and goes back into the room. The room smells damp and husky, like nobody has been in there for years. Agnes slowly guides herself around the room with her hand stroking against the wall. For the first ten or so steps Agnes takes, all she can see is the black wall paint. But then her fingers touch a bump on the wall, so she raises her candle in front of where she felt the bump to see what exactly it is. GASP. Agnes gasps, squeals under her breath and tightly clenches her eyes. What she has seen is something tremendously disturbing. A framed painting of limbless little boy Edward laid on the ice bath in the bathroom after his arms and limbs had been severed. Agnes' stomach turns and she turns a pale shade of blue. She opens her eyes and looks for a plaque to see who had painted the painting. She spots a plaque just below the painting, reading 'Mary Dwendle - 1662.' Agnes' eyes bulge, but it is no surprise to her, since the witches are the ones who in fact killed the thirteen year old altar boy. She slowly lifts her hand up to the painting and strokes it against Edward's face.

"You're at peace now, with the Lord. I am so sorry that the church failed so miserably to protect you from this vile attack. I shall always keep you and your family in my prayers, justice will be served very soon" says Agnes as her eyes begin to swell up with tears. She gulps and continues to stroll around the room, after this one painting of Edward there are more and more paintings on the wall, all painted by Mary. This room is Mary's art exhibition room.

"What kind of sick human being takes pleasure in painting such horrific images" she whispers. Then her foot bangs into something, so she takes a step back and shines her candle in front of her. What she sees is an easel, holding Mary's next piece of artwork. The girl, half painted on the canvas, is their latest victim, the eleven year old girl that they drank the blood of just earlier on that very morning.

"Good lord, how can anybody be so sick?" Says Agnes out loud before storming out of the room, closing the door, blowing out her candle and brushing herself off. She decides that she now wants to venture upstairs to see what else she can find. She climbs up the grand staircase to the third floor and sees the first door of the corridor on her right hand side. This door is the odd one out as it is painted red instead of black. Agnes is now ever so curious to see what is behind the closed door. She walks over to the red door and turns the doorknob one hundred and eighty degrees until it clicks and the door opens a tiny little bit. Through the tiny crevasse at the side of the door, Agnes can see that there is just a wooden floor and a wooden toilet.

"Huh. I just could do with going to the toilet" huffs Agnes to herself as she opens the door wider. She doesn't check the rest of the room, she just walks straight on over to the toilet, lifts up her petticoat and sits on the toilet seat.

"Ahhhh" moans Agnes, as she closes her eyes and releases her urine. She then opens her eyes.

"OH MY GOODNESS! OH MY GOODNESS!! OH MY GOODNESS!!!" Screams Agnes as her face drops.

"WHAT IN SATAN'S NAME IS THIS?!" She continues to yell. In Front of Agnes at the opposite side of the room is the bath where the fresh corpses are kept on ice. Agnes quickly lifts herself from the toilet and puts her petticoat back down. She goes over to the bathtub and looks over.

"Oh my, poor little girl" says Agnes blubbering and shaking from the shock. Meanwhile Agnes is in shock over the dead body of the eleven year old girl whom the witches had sucked the blood out of, Rose hears Agnes' screaming and starts to walk up the stairs to see what is the matter. She barged into the bathroom, slamming the door against the wall.

"What is all this screaming? I'm trying to read a book downstairs and all I can hear is your yelling and it's driving me crazy!" Says Rose.

"WHAT IS THIS! This is disgusting! Horrifying!" Screams Agnes.

"PLEASE. Stop screaming already! Welcome to the bathroom, this is where our corpses lay on ice until we eat their flesh and drink their blood" replies Rose.

"Poor, poor girl. May the lord be with you" says Agnes, making the sign of the cross. Rose laughs.

"Do you like the red door, Agnes? Mary used the finest paint in this town, she has always been quite the artist" says Rose. Agnes crunches her knuckles, knowing very well that Mary is quite the artist after seeing her paintings, but knows that she shouldn't mention to anybody that she has seen them.

"Ah yes, blood. Such a nice colour isn't it? If I remember correctly it was from one of our first victims shortly after we moved into this house. A little boy. I still remember the taste of…" says Rose.

"ENOUGH!" Agnes interrupts, covering her ears.

"I really would like nothing more other than to just go to a room where I could rest. Please could you show me to one?" She continues.

"Of course! You need plenty of rest for tomorrow anyway. Follow me" says Rose as she begins to walk down the corridor. Agnes follows her as they go down the stairs to the second floor. Rose knocks on the door of the first room on the corridor to see if the room is vacant or not. There is so reply to the knock so Rose opens the door. Inside the room, there is just a mattress on the cold, hard, wooden floor.

"Doesn't it remind you of the first night you spent with us here, Agnes?" Laughs Rose. Agnes ignores her snarky remark and just walks into the room.

"This should be fine, thank you" says Agnes.

"Well, have a little rest, but then be ready, for it is the blood moon tonight. It happens only on the odd occasion. It is quite spectacular. For us witches it is a special time, so we like to celebrate. We will all be going into the garden at around 3am when the red moon should be visible at around 3:30am. I shall come to get you" says Rose.

"Thank you" says Agnes. Rose leaves the room and goes back downstairs to read her book. Agnes lays on the mattress and quickly drifts off to sleep.

Chapter Sixteen
BLOOD MOON

Downstairs, Fiona is preparing the food and garden for the blood moon celebration.

Whilst everything is now calm inside the coven, things are just heating up in the Southbrook town church.

"Higher! Lower! Little bit higher!" Shouts Father Elliot. The people of the church have created a hammock - like contraption made out of silk that hangs from the ceiling and when a rope is pulled the material drops. BANG. The church door bangs open.

"I'm back! Could some of you come and help me fetch all of the salt inside? It's starting to rain out there!" Says the man who travelled to Nickleded for the salt. Three of the church goers go outside to get the salt to bring back into the church.

He has brought back ten huge sacks of pure sea salt on his carriage. They each grab a sack and throw it over their shoulder to take inside, then going back out to grab another sack until all of the salt has been offloaded. Father Elliot pulls the rope and drops the material back down so that the salt can be scattered onto the silk to prepare the trap.

"Okay, thank you. Now, let's all grab a sack of salt and pour it evenly over the silk, then I can put the silk back up to the ceiling ready for the morning" says Father Elliot. Ten of the church goers, including Father Elliot grab a sack of the salt, tear open the top and pour over the white silk material. After the salt is all scattered on the silk, Father Elliot pulls the rope to lift up the material to the roof of the church, where the witches would never notice it, or even if they did, they would never know what it is holding.

"Ha! They have no idea what they have coming" laughs Father Elliot.

"Let's leave it here for today then, you may all go on home. Just remember to be here at 10am so that we can get set up. I'll light the candles, so that it looks like mass is on. Julie, you can even play the piano as if we are waiting to begin! Then the rest of us can wait in the chapel, next to the rope, waiting for the witches and Sister Agnes to enter, then we drop the salt all over these wretched satanists, sending them back to where they belong... hell" says Father Elliot cunningly. All of the church goers go home and Father Elliot makes his way back to the Parish where he can relax and reflect on his and Agnes' perfect plan and anticipate the morning.

It is now the early hours of the morning. KNOCK. KNOCK. KNOCK. Rose bangs on the door of the room where Agnes is sleeping. She then turns the black painted door knob, opens the door and enters.

"Rose, it's so early, what is going on?" Says Agnes, squinting her eyes and stretching her legs.

"Ugh, it stinks in here" says Rose. Agnes lays her head back down on the mattress and huffs.

"No time for resting, Agnes. Look out the window" says Rose. Agnes turns her head to the side, crunching her neck.

"Wow. Everything is so... red!" Says Agnes. Outside the window, everything is a hewy red because of the blood moon.

"Yes, now look up to the moon" Rose continues. Agnes gets up from the mattress and hobbles over to the window to see the moon.

"It is so red! Some kind of evil. God did not have a control over this! SATAN! IT IS SATAN'S MOON! OH MY, I MUST PRAY THAT IT GOES AWAY" blubbers Agnes.

"Oh shush, old lady. It goes away, don't worry. But us witches believe that it is a rejuvenating time for our souls. So, like I mentioned earlier, we are having a little bit of a party. Shake off this sleepiness and come with me down stairs" says Rose. Agnes rubs both of her eyes and begins to follow Rose out of the room.

"What kind of party must you have for a moon?" Questions Agnes.

"Oh... you will see" grins Rose wickedly whilst walking in front of Agnes down the stairs. They both go down to the first floor, where they are greeted by Edith and Mary at the bottom of the staircase.

"Ah, Agnes is joining the party!" Says Mary.

"Woohoo! Come outside Rose, we need to finish what we have started before the moon returns to its normal state" says Edith.

"Okay" says Rose, grabbing Agnes' shoulder and guiding her into the kitchen towards the garden door. Agnes walks past Fiona, who is busy cooking something in the kitchen. She then gets a glimpse of what is outside through the window.

"Wait" she mumbles.

"What?" Asks Rose.

"What is that?" Agnes continues.

"Just follow us, all will be revealed" replies Rose. Mary and Edith cackle as they open the garden door. Rose guides Agnes to the open door frame, standing behind her.

"OH MY!!" Screams Agnes hysterically.

"LET ME BACK INSIDE" she continuously screams as she struggles to get out of Roses' arms, trying to turn around to go back inside the house.

"They say that the blood moon is rejuvenating. So, it is obviously the best time for us witches to drink the virgin blood. It will have twice the effect!" Says Mary.

"Yes and you certainly need it, Mary" says Rose. Mary bows her head in shame.

"THIS MONSTROSITY! RELEASE HIM RIGHT AWAY!" Screams Agnes.

"Just step outside" says Edith.

"NO" yells Agnes, still struggling.

"YES!" Shouts Edith, dragging her into the garden.

"You live here now! You follow our rules" says Mary.

"Just sit here and watch, you don't have to participate" says Rose, sitting Agnes into a wooden chair in the garden. Agnes sits, shaking with her eyes closed. What stands before her is a young virgin church boy, roped cruelly to a large tree.

"SISTER AGNES! OH MY GOODNESS, SISTER AGNES! IS THAT YOU? YOU MUST HELP ME! THEY ARE GOING TO KILL ME!" Shouts the young boy with a sense of unsure relief.

"MY CHILD! THERE IS NOTHING I CAN DO! GOODNESS! RELEASE HIM RIGHT NOW!" Agnes continues to scream as she runs up to the boy fastly to try and help him. WHOOSH. Edith snaps her fingers and slides Agnes back into her chair. Agnes is terrified.

"SILENCE! EVERYONE! SHUT UP YOUNG BOY, OR ELSE WE CAN THINK OF SOMETHING MUCH WORSE TO PUT YOU OUT OF YOUR MISERY. AS FOR YOU, AGNES, JUST STAY SEATED" shouts Edith, losing her temper.

"He will be fresh meat soon. Then Fiona can add his flesh into the delicious soup which she is preparing right now for us for us all to enjoy. We also figured that since you won't be drinking the blood, you'll need some protein and vitamins inside you too, we don't want you to be so malnourished, so the soup should be just the thing to spruce you up" says Rose. Agnes sits in her chair, helpless, screaming at the top of her lungs along with the young boy, clawing her hands and scratching them on her head in terror.

"Blood moon, blood moon, we will drink the blood soon. Keep us youthful, beautiful, sinful. Slit the neck, feel the breathe, it'll be his final one, for then shortly later will come the blazing sun" chant Rose, Edith, Mary and the other witches in unison.

SPLISH. SPLASH. SLERP. Rose breaks the chant, smiles insanely, pulls out a butchers knife from her apron and slits the young boys' neck whilst performing a psychotic dance, spinning around and skipping side to side. After she has slit his neck right through to the bone, his blood sprays out and he is killed instantly. The witches fight with each other, trying to suck the most blood directly out of his neck as they possibly can. They each press their mouths against his neck, roughly around five times each, sucking and slurping hard for the blood, until it ends on Mary's turn when there is no more blood squirting from his neck. Now they all stand around the bloody corpse chanting five times "Blood moon, blood moon, we have drank the blood now. We will be youthful, beautiful, sinful. We slit the neck, felt his breath, it was is final one. Now, we wait for the blazing sun." Meanwhile, Agnes sits paralysed with her mouth dropped down, her body shaking and her eyes fixated on the body. The witches, covered in blood, go back into the house to clean themselves up. Agnes, now alone in the garden, steps out of her paralysed state and decides to go over to the body. Blubbering uncontrollably and her eyes blurred by her tears, she strokes the hair on his bowed head, expressing her sorrow. BANG. Agnes is interrupted and runs back to her seat when Rose bangs open the door holding a saw in her hand and all of the witches run back into the garden like hooligans.

"Fiona is ready for the meat" says Rose psychotically as she skips towards the corpse with the saw in her hand, smiling and drooling at the mouth like she is no longer a human. Agnes screams loudly and clenches her eyes shut. The sound is haunting and deeply disturbing when Rose begins to saw into the young boy's arm, amputating it from the shoulder. She saws through both of his arms and legs, then picks up the members and lobs them over her left shoulder before taking them into the kitchen and laying them on the table for Fiona to prepare and add into the soup.

"Slice off the tenderest pieces of meat" says Rose to Fiona.

"Yes, madam" says Fiona feeling uneasy. She rolls over one of the legs to get a grip on the thigh, she then squints her eyes, picks up a butcher's knife and begins to cut away the flesh from the thigh. When Fiona has cut all of the meat off and all that is left is the bone, she lays the meat as flatly as possible on the table and begins to dice small chunks of the flesh. Then, she lightly sautées the flesh and adds some salt for flavour, she tosses and turns the flesh in the frying pan until golden brown on the outside yet still bloody on the inside. Lastly, she adds the half cooked flesh into the large stock pan that she has hanging over the fire to slowly finish off cooking with the soup. After Fiona has done this, she must carry the remaining arms and leg up to the bathroom on the third floor to preserve them on ice until the witches wish to eat the meat or drain some more blood. She lifts up the limbs with a disgusted look on her face, the smell of the flesh is so potent that she gips, but she carries the arms and leg all the way up to the bathroom on the third floor, then goes back downstairs and cleans up the kitchen. Back in the garden, the witches are now all cleaned up and are just sat having a casual chat.

"How could you be so evil?" Whispers Agnes with trembling voice.

"Listen, all of the catholics are going to be wiped out tomorrow, so you better get used to this. Otherwise, we can find our own way there and you can stay here" says Rose.

"No, no... no! Ha! It's fine. Just, something different for me, that's all" replies Agnes.

"Soup is ready!" Shouts Fiona with her head sticking through the garden door.

"Yum! Come on ladies! Fill up your bowl" says Mary, leading the witches and Agnes through the door into the kitchen. Agnes' stomach turns, however she now knows that she must be on her best behaviour in order to be let out to the church tomorrow, so, she smiles and pretends to be one with the witches, just for one last night. She receives the cup of freshly sautéed virgin flesh and pretends to be graceful.

"Thank you very much, mmm, smells delightful!" Lies Agnes.

"Great. She's slowly becoming one of us ladies! Must be something about this blood moon" laughs Rose.

"Now, I would love to make a toast! This past week has been filled with so much excitement. First, I had the thrill of catching Agnes. Sorry Agnes, it was fun though. Now, she has lead us to finally defeating the catholics and then us witches can run this town and slowly turn the whole of England into a witch-only country. It's what I've always dreamt of since I discovered my powers. Tomorrow my dream, our dream, will finally become reality. Cheers, ladies. Let's have this soup and then go to bed, for it will be an action packed day tomorrow. Once again, cheers!" Rose toasts. She holds her cup out to the witches and they all clink their cup against it, she holds her cup out to Agnes and Agnes cracks a fake smile and giggle and clinks her cup against Rose's.

"I'm just so glad I'll be serving my lord again. Clearly if they never came to help me, then they are not true catholics at all. They knew I was in danger, or missing, and they never bothered to even so much as look for me. So now, justice will be served" says Agnes.

"Ah, wonderful. I can hear their skin burning already, what a soothing and blissful sound. Come on ladies, let's take a sip" says Edith. Rose nods in agreement. All of the witches raise their glass to their mouth and take a sip, Agnes watches with a sour look on her face.

"Is there something wrong now, Agnes?" Asks Mary.

"No, no. Not at all! I was just daydreaming about how good it is going to feel to annihilate them tomorrow" she cackles. She then lifts the cup up to her mouth, then with her hand shaking and her nostrils flaring, she takes a sip, when she takes the sip she accidentally allows a chunk of flesh into her mouth. Agnes gags forcefully with disgust.

"Whatever is the matter?" Asks Rose.

"Oh, nothing. Nothing at all. It just went down the wrong hole" gasps Agnes.

"Well just be careful with the rest!" Replies Rose. Agnes smiles and holds her cup up again. They all slurp the soup and then put their cups on the table.

"Right, okay, well then that's it! Let's go to sleep and await the morning sun. It feels so good knowing that they will all be gone by noon. What a spectacular feeling" laughs Rose as she and the witches walk away to go to their rooms and sleep. Agnes stays behind in the kitchen and as soon as the witches are out of sight and she can no longer hear them, she rushes to the sink and spews all of the soup back up.

"DISGUSTING!" She shouts under her breath as she wipes the spew from around her mouth.

Chapter Seventeen
STRUGGLING TO PRAY

Fiona enters the kitchen after doing some cleaning in the living room. She tucks her duster into the pocket of her apron.

"So, are you ready for tomorrow?" Asks Fiona, with an unsure look on her face.

"You know how dangerous this is for us, right? We are taking a very big risk here" she continues. Agnes turns around from the sink to converse with Fiona.

"We mustn't worry. Father Elliot and the church goers will have everything under control. All me and you must do is stick together, stay next to me when we get to the church, then we can help along with the church goers to put them all to their death" says Agnes in a comforting voice.

"Shush! Shush! What if the witches are still lingering. We shouldn't talk about this. It isn't safe. I will just stay by your side tomorrow. Should we say a quiet prayer together?" Expresses Fiona.

"Of course, let's say the Hail Mary" says Agnes, closing her eyes and putting her hands together.

"Stop! Keep your eyes open, just in case one of them comes down the stairs, so you can see them" says Fiona.

"Okay, my eyes are wide open. Could you lead the prayer?" Asks Agnes.

"Of course. Hail Mary… oh my goodness" gasps Fiona.

"What happened? Did you hear somebody come downstairs?" Asks Agnes.

"No. I can't remember what's next Agnes!" Says a Frantic and disturbed Fiona.

"Oh my. What kind of catholic are you!" Says Agnes, with a disgusted look on her face.

"It's the strangest thing. Agnes, I say this prayer every night before I sleep. But now for some unknown reason to me, I cannot remember for the life of me what is after Hail Mary, my mind just goes so blank!" She expresses.

"Okay, well then I will lead the prayer. Hail Mary... OH MY GOODNESS! WHAT ON EARTH IS THIS! I CANNOT REMEMBER EITHER. IT IS ALMOST AS IF I NEVER KNEW THE PRAYER" shouts Agnes in distress.

"SHUSH!" Shouts Fiona under her breath, grabbing Agnes lips and pressing them together.

"I am panicking. Let's try another one. Our Father... OH DEAR! I CAN'T REMEMBER THAT ONE EITHER!" Shouts Agnes under her breath with her veins bulging out of her now blushed neck.

"They must have put a spell on us, a curse, they're trying to pull us on to the dark side now, they must be wiser about this whole plan than we think. Maybe they are wiser than we think and they know that we will turn against them tomorrow! So they're trying to alter our minds, trying to turn us into one of them! Agnes we have no way of stopping this evil! What can we do?!" Cries Fiona.

"Okay, don't panic, we still have our faith. We still remember our bible and our Lord, that is all we need. Just hold onto that as tightly as possible. They can never take away the lord from me no matter what spell or potion they smother onto me. The lord is half of me, they would psychically have to cut me in half to get the lord out of me!" Says Agnes, calmly bending down to distressed Fiona.

"Be careful what you say! I wouldn't put it past them to cut you in half. They are quite used to cutting people up as you have very well seen, Agnes" says Fiona, continuing to blubber.

"Listen, you must be strong. The Lord is looking out for us anyway. His love is so much stronger than any spell. We WILL be okay. It is only tomorrow. They couldn't strip us of our holiness in only a few hours even if they tried their hardest!" Says Agnes holding Fiona's shaking hands.

"Okay, I trust you, just please help me out of this place. I want to be free again" says Fiona, wiping up her tears.

"Go to sleep, get ready for tomorrow and remember to just stay by my side" says Agnes, smiling peacefully.

"Okay, good night sweet Agnes. God bless you" says Fiona, sniffling and turning around to go up to bed.

"God bless you, too. Sleep well" says Agnes. Fiona turns her head and smiles with her eyes still wet, before continuing towards the staircase.

Chapter Eighteen
PLANS IN ACTION

DING.

DING.

DING.

It is Sunday morning. The church bells ring. Over in the Coven, Agnes awakes. She rubs her tired, puffy eyes and releases a tremendous yawn. She shakes her head fast. "Ah! Today is the big day" she says to herself with a giddiness in her tone.

At the Church, Father Elliot has started to let people in. "Come on in, come on in, take a seat, you're safe here." He says to the people coming in with a big smile.

Back in the Coven. "WITCHES, WITCHES, WAKE UP! TODAY IS THE DAY WE TAKE OVER!" Shouts an overly happy and excited Rose, strolling through the corridors of the house banging a spoon against a saucepan. "What on earth is that noise?" Says Agnes, covering her ears and standing to leave her room. She opens her door, steps outside and sees Rose with her saucepan and spoon. "ROSE! Please, I am going to have a headache!" She Shouts. Rose looks to Agnes and Shouts "ah! Agnes! You're the first one awake! Brilliant, come down, get ready, we're setting off soon. I'll come up and wake the others." She walks up the stairs and goes to every single room and bangs on the doors, waking the witches. "COME ON! IT'S FINALLY TIME!" She Shouts. Agnes sighs and walks down the stairs and takes a seat in the kitchen. Around thirty minutes after Rose's wake up call, all of the witches start making their way downstairs and into the hallway. "OKAY! EVERYONE LINE UP! Let's make sure we're all here and there's nobody missing out on today's luxury by sleeping!" Shouts Rose. "So, we have myself, Edith, Mary, Agnes, Fiona and … 1,2,3,4,5.. umm yeah, too many to count, I am sure we're all here" she says. "Let's all join hands! Let's all take just one moment together, of pride and achievement" says Edith. All of the witches smile at each other and join hands. Fiona and Agnes roll their eyeballs to the side to catch each other's eyes, smile and join hands with the witches, knowing exactly what is going to take place. "OKAY! COME ON! WE ARE GOING!" Shouts Rose. The witches all roar and start stomping their way to the door to exit and make their ways to the church. "WAIT" yells Agnes. Everybody turns around. "Umm, the clock! Look at the clock! It is only nine o'clock! Mass doesn't fully start until nine thirty usually. Let's give it time, so everybody is surely in the church, otherwise there could still be people on the streets that are gonna see us!" She continues. "Hmmm, maybe you have a point" replies Rose. "Ladies, go back in line, we will give it five more minutes" says Mary. Agnes doesn't care about how the witches benefit, she is just biding time for everyone in the town to get to the church so that they will be safe and so that the plan is fully in working action. Five minutes pass, Rose picks up her heavy wheel of tied up rope which she will use to tie the catholic's to trees and tells everybody to start making their way out. "COME ON, LET'S GO, BUT ALL STICK TOGETHER! AGNES WILL LEAD THE WAY! Since she is the one who has attended the church for the past 100 years" sniggers Rose. "How funny" says Agnes whilst scowling. "FOLLOW ME!" She says, whilst grabbing Fiona and bringing her to the front of the mob with her. "How are you feeling?" She Asks Fiona. Fiona has a tear streaming down her cheek. "Oh Agnes, it's been so long since I have seen anything other than that old Coven! I forgot how beautiful God's creation really was. I just can't wait to have my life back. Thank you so much Agnes, you truly are a saint set to go straight to the best spot in heaven" She blubbers. "Well, you will be right there next to me" replies Agnes, smiling at Fiona in reassurance. They both giggle and continue to make their way to the church. At the back of the mob, Mary, Edith and Rose are having their own private conversations too. "Just be very careful, everything is going well so far, but if anything does go wrong, we have our powers remember, just set fire to the church" says Rose. Edith and Mary nod their heads in agreement.

"Well, well, we'll… the time has come! Here we are, ladies! Here is the church!" Agnes says to the witches, before turning around and really sinking in the image of the church that she loves so much. She grabs Fiona's hand and they both shed a tear. "SHHHH! Everyone, we must be quiet, otherwise they may hear us! Remember the plan. I'll knock on the door, then Agnes will do her thing. Then, we grab them by their arms, legs, necks, genitals… whatever! Just grab them, bring them outside, then leave the rest to me!" Says Rose with an excited tremor in her voice. "God, my palms are sweaty because I'm so excited!" Says Mary. "Here we go! I love you all" are Rose's last words before she knocks three times on the door. KNOCK, KNOCK, KNOCK.

Inside the Church, Father Elliot and the people of the town fastly turn around towards the door. Father Elliot gulps a ball in his throat, signals for everyone to be quiet and plays out his own plan. "Oh, everyone, I think there must be some more people who want to join our mass today! Allow me to answer the door" he says loudly enough for the witches outside to hear, so that they won't suspect anything. On the outside, Rose's face lights up with delight. Father Elliot clears his throat, whispers for everyone to get in their places and for a church member to stand with the string and to pull it exactly five seconds after the witches enter the building, to allow the salt to drop on them and eliminate their powers. He strolls to the door, closes his eyes for a second, prays to God that it all goes to plan and then slowly reaches out his hand to the door knob. He twists it and the door bangs open. Agnes and Father Elliot are finally in each other's company again. Agnes greatly fights the urge to smile at Father Elliot because she must act like an enemy in order for the plan to work. So, Father Elliot makes the first move. "AGNES. OH MY GOOD LORD, IS IT REALLY YOU? WHERE HAVE YOU BEEN? OH I HAVE MISSED YOU SO MUCH! COME ON IN! I see you have brought some more people! The more the merrier! Come on in!" Shouts an overly happy and animated Father Elliot. "HOW COULD YOU! HOW COULD YOU NOT EVEN LOOK FOR ME! THE LORD WILL BE SO ASHAMED OF YOU! YOUR UNHOLINESS WILL NOT GO UNSEEN! NOW IT IS YOUR TURN TO GO MISSING, BUT FOR YOU, OH NO, YOU WON'T BE COMING BACK! YOU ARE GOING STRAIGHT TO HELL!" Shouts an aggressive Agnes. "Now, now, now Agnes! Please! It isn't how it seems, come on, come inside, bring your new friends and we can sort this out!" Replies Father Elliot.

Agnes nods her head in agreement and takes a step into the building. Everything is still silent. Agnes has now crossed over from the witches, back to the good side, with her people, it has been so long since she saw the inside of the church, smelt and touched it too, she is overwhelmed and tears up again. "Agnes, we didn't agree to this! Come back out here!" Says Rose, with a fake smile so that Father Elliot will not notice anything going on. "No, it's fine, we can enter, we and Father Elliot will have words, while you sit and pray" says Agnes. "Oh, okay! I guess that is what we shall do then, ladies! Come on in, we wanted to say our prayers anyway. How wonderful is this building" says Rose, leading the pack of witches into the church. Father Elliot fastly closes the door, Agnes stands aside, the witches all huddle together. The door has been closed for exactly five short seconds, which for Agnes and Father Elliot felt like forever. The man stood with the string pulls hard and groans loudly. Nothing happens. "What is going on?" Asks Rose, still fake smiling. Agnes' stomach churns. "Oh, umm, it's a new tradition! Whenever somebody enters the church now, the Church bells must be rung! We see it as kind of like letting God know that we have entered his home. "Keep pulling! It'll work eventually!" Shouts Agnes to the man, with a tremor in her voice.

Chapter Nineteen
FLABBERGASTED WITCHES

The man pulls again. This time it works. The witches
look up to the roof, everything is all in slow motion, the
fabric falls ever so delicately, a break of sunlight appears
through the window and the salt begins to fall. It is all
very fast but appears so slow. The people sat in the
church gasp and turn around to look at the witches, the
witches cover their heads and drop to the ground, Agnes
smiles at Father Elliot and he smiles back. All in a few
seconds. Then, the slow motion wears off. The witches
begin to scream. Before the salt hit Edith, she even used
her powers to set fire to the front of the church. Father
Elliot runs to put out the fire, Sister Agnes instructs the
people of the church to all grab a witch. "AGNES!
AGNES! WHAT IS THIS! I DO NOT UNDERSTAND!
IT WAS ALL GOING SO WELL! I AM GONNA KILL
YOU!" Screams Rose, pouncing onto Agnes. Agnes
Screams for help. One of the church goers runs up to
help, smacks Rose in the face, knocking her out. Agnes
rises from the ground and gets back onto her feet.
"GRAB THEM, GRAB THEM!" She shouts from the
top of her lungs. All the members of the church grab the
witches and pull their arms behind their backs and cross
their wrists over so they cannot move. They wriggle and
scream but could not be released no matter how hard
they tried, the people of the church were determined to

kill the witches, in return for the killings of their loved ones. Sister Agnes, once more, proudly swings open the huge door of her beloved Church, sniffs in the fresh air and watches as her enemies are dragged out and taken to the trees. Everybody now leaves the church, Agnes closes the door and makes her way over to the trees, the church people are tying the witches to the trees. "Bliss. Heaven. That is what this is" Agnes cackles. "THIS WAS NOT THE PLAN! I CANNOT BELIEVE YOU BETRAYED US ALL LIKE THIS!" Screams Edith. "To see you all tied up and help against your will, just like I once was by you, is bliss. BURN THEM" continues Agnes. "GET THE WINE, AGNES!" Shouts Father Elliot. Agnes gasps. "Perfect idea! We can burn the witches as they are soaked in the blood of Christ! The ultimate repentance for these witches." She snarls as she runs back into the church to find the canister of sacramental wine. She holds it in her arms and blesses it by kissing it and saying a quick prayer. "May this blessed wine rinse the witches of their heavy and troubled souls and send them to wherever they must go" whispers Agnes before gulping and running out the doors of the church. "WITCHES, AT YOUR STEAKS, MEET YOUR DEATH!" Shouts Agnes as she psychotically skips around the trees. The church attendees stand back and watch as if it is all a movie. Half of their reaction is of shock horror, then of course the rest is of bliss, knowing that the witches will no longer be of trouble to them, their homes or families. Agnes starts going around the witches one by one and douses them in the red wine. "EW! WHAT IS THIS" Shouts Rose. "This, Rose, is the blood of Christ, the blood of he who shall heal you for all of your wrong doings." Explains Agnes. Agnes splashes some of the wine in Rose's mouth. Rose spits it back out onto Agnes' face. Agnes wipes her face with her grimey, old and wrinkled fingers and splats the saliva onto the ground. SLAP. Agnes slaps Rose across her cheek. "I HAVE THE POWER NOW! You can spit it out, but Christ will forever be inside of you now." Says a raging Agnes. She continues to slowly stroll amongst the witches and soak them in the wine, until it is time. Time for the witches to burn. "ANY LAST WORDS?" Shouts Agnes. All of the witches' screams combine to make a haunting howling noise. Father Elliot hands Sister Agnes a match and the pack of matches for her to strike it against. She takes a deep breath of vindication and pride and then pulls the match against the box. The flame glows. A tear shaped burning hot flame, ready to burn the most powerful witches in Southbrook. She throws the match directly at Rose. "Enjoy your time with the devil, I'm sure you will get along just fine." She says with a cunning grin on her face. All in one second, Rose's whole body is engulfed in flames, she screams so piercingly loud. The fire spreads, from witch to witch, as Agnes, Father Elliot and all of the Catholic stand back and watch. Observing everything that goes against their religion being burnt into ashes, their eyes gleam with happiness and purity, comfort and great joy.

The witches, who were once untouchable, are now deceased and furthermore, just a pile of unholy ashes. Agnes turns to Fiona.

"I told you we'd do it! How does it feel to be free?" She asks.

"Oh, my goodness, I still can't really believe it. I am no longer a slave to these witches, I am free, I can go to church, sing and dance, just finally be happy!" Screeches Fiona with tears in her eyes as she does a little happy dance. Agnes then turns to Father Elliot, they look at each other with such serenity and then hug.

"It's good to have you back, Agnes" says Father Elliot, with tears welling up in his eyes.

"Well, I can most definitely say that this has been the best day of my life, now I just can't wait to attend mass tomorrow and for normality to be restored." She replies. They both take one last look at the piles of ashes before them, smile and turn away. Agnes steps back into the church and exhales deeply. "Ahhhhh! I missed the smell. I missed my lord. My home, I am finally home." Says a very joyful Agnes.

Chapter Twenty
SOUTHBROOK SAVED

It is now the day after.

Agnes awakes in the nunnery, after a blissful first night back in her holy accommodation. She yawns loudly, gets up from her bed, dresses herself in a fresh habit and then sets off to the Church for morning mass.

She stands at the front of the Church, conversing with Father Elliot as the sacred building fills up with the people of Southbrook. In single file formation, they trickle into the Church one by one, gobsmacked to see Sister Kirktrut's return. "Goodness, she's back!" Shouts out one lady. Everything is silent and eerie.

Agnes calmly walks her way up to the pulpit and cracks her knuckles.

"Well, hello! Good morning to you all. As you can see, I am indeed back to where I belong. It has been a very tumultuous and reacher strange time in my life. As I am sure you have all been told, yes, I was being held captive by witches. They held me captive, forced me to see things that I will never forget, one of them even tried to seduce me." She says passionately whilst thumping the wood with her leathery old fist. "But yesterday, through my lord I was rescued. Father Elliot, a lot of you people sat before me and myself burnt the witches. They are now deceased, a pile of wretched ash, gone and can no longer be of any harm to us or our town. Contrary to mine and Father Elliot's previous beliefs, it was indeed confirmed that it was in fact the witches who caused those catastrophic events that happened a couple of months ago. Oh and I can only humbly apologise for what I have done to some of your loved ones, but I was just trying to serve the lord in doing what I felt was correct. Now that I have gotten rid of these witches, I will be forgiven by the Lord." She continues in a confident and powerful tone. She clears her throat.

"I would now like to ask Father Elliot to come and stand by me, as I say a few words."

Father Elliot strolls up to the pulpit and stands by Agnes' side.

"Father, how could I ever thank you enough, for all you have done to save me" says Agnes with tears in her eyes. "Well, we all just couldn't wait to have you back at the church Agnes, it just didn't feel the same without your holy presence." Replies Father Elliot, smiling with pride.

"Thank you Father, now let us pray. You may all close your eyes." Says Agnes, smiling back. As instructed, everybody in the audience and Father Elliot close their eyes. Agnes says that she will now light a candle to bring them all closer to the Lord. She reaches out her long, veiny, scrawny arm, grabs the metal candle holder from one of the side tables, then in a fit of rage she strikes Father Elliot around the head with it. BANG. Everybody's eyes open faster than the speed of light, there are gasps and screams as they see Father Elliot laid on the floor of the alter with blood gushing from his head. However, he is still conscious.

"AGNES, PLEASE, WHAT HAS GOTTEN INTO YOU, WHAT IS THIS ABOUT! I THOUGHT YOU

WERE HAPPY TO BE BACK AT THE CHURCH!"
Screams a terrified Father Elliot.

"COWARD!" Shouts Agnes with an evil growl in her
tone.

The crowd is stunned. Father Elliot tries to shuffle his
body away from Agnes but she just comes closer and
closer and then steps on his garments so that he can no
longer crawl away.

"YOU LEFT ME! LEFT ME WITH THOSE
WITCHES! YOU KNEW THAT I WAS THERE AND
YOU JUST LEFT ME ALONE! God has no time for
traitors, just like Judas, you gave me the kiss of death.
Only in this story, I AM THE ONE WHO SURVIVES!"
Yells Agnes.

"Agnes it's not true!" Pleads Father Elliot.

"ENOUGH! You are useless to this church, I will make
a much better leader for these people! This town will be
restored to its once great level of holiness." Continues
Agnes, smiling from ear to ear. Her smile turns into a
satanic grin. She bends down to Father Elliot, slaps her
skeletal hands onto his shoulders and drags him across
the wooden floor over to the font, which is used to dunk
infants into holy water during a baptism. She whips his
body with her hands ordering him to stand. Father Elliot
grabs onto the font with both hands and pulls himself up.
He stands there, breathless with his bloodied head
hovering over the font, staring at the reflection of

himself in the holy water. Blood starts to drip into the water, Father Elliot cries.

"You have finally met your destiny. I know that this is what my Lord would want me to do" grumbles Agnes. She Grabs him once more as the audience screams in horror. "Here we go! Straight to hell! Straight to hell!" She screams as she forces Father Elliot's head into the font causes the holy liquid to overspill and splash all over the wooden floor. Father Elliot is trying to fight back but he can't get his footing right on the wet slippery floor, he is just hopelessly wriggling around like an insect. Agnes raises his head back up from the font, to let him have his final breath. Father Elliot, now blue in the face takes a ginormous gasp of air. Agnes then grabs the back of his hair to force his head back down.

But all of a sudden...

SMASH!

Silence.

Gasps.

In one split second, everything changes.

Fiona, who was sitting in the audience watching the whole ordeal unfold took fast action. Whilst Agnes was possessed in her moment of power, she crawled behind her, then stood up and gently unhooked one of the large, gold framed paintings from the wall of the church. Just before Agnes was about to slam Father Elliot's head back into the font, she lifted the large painting and smacked it down onto Sister Agnes. The golden frame struck the top of her head, her skull cracked open. Agnes layed there… deceased.

Everybody swarms around Father Elliot, making sure he is okay, they stomp over Agnes' body, as if she is just a sack of rubbish. Father Elliot is seated in a chair and is given a glass of cold water, he takes a gulp and then closes his eyes, trying to get his breath back.

Fiona is sat on the floor sobbing, feeling guilty for killing Sister Agnes.

 "Oh God! What have I done!" She sobs. The people of the church remind her that she did what she had to do, they thank her for it. If Fiona didn't kill Agnes, who knows what could've happened to the town. It would have been a town run by a monster. Fiona slowly comes to peace with herself and decides that killing Agnes was what was necessary, she couldn't let her kill the head of the church, Fiona was just too holy to let that happen.

 "We should leave Father Elliot to rest" says one of the church goers. They all agree, and make their way out of the church and back to their homes. Fiona stays and takes Father Elliot to a back room in the church to rest. She seats him, fills up his glass of water and then weeps.

"Dear, why are you sobbing?" Asks Father Elliot.

"I killed someone, Father, the lord will never forgive me!" Cries Fiona.

"An eye for an eye, she got what she deserved, I think in the end being locked away with those witches just got into her head. Anyway, she is gone now there is nothing we can do" replies Father Elliot. Fiona pats her eyes and smiles.

"Well I guess we should move her body somewhere though" says Fiona.

"Yes, let's lay her to rest. We can dig a hole in the back churchyard and patch her over nicely" suggest Father Elliot.

"But Father, aren't you feeling weak after what happened?" Asks Fiona.

"Not anymore, I feel healthy now, come, follow me" Father Elliot stands from his chair, sways a little and then guides Fiona to the back churchyard. The pouring rain rinses the blood from Father Elliot's head. They each take a spade and dig up a grave for Agnes. They then go back into the church to get her. She lays there, clothed in shattered fragments of the painting that was smashed over her head, bloodied from the blow. Her skin pasty, eyes empty and evil gone. Fiona grabs her feet, Father Elliot grabs her wrists and they gently walk her through the back of the church and into the yard. They then lower her body into the grave they have dug.

"Good night, Agnes. I am not sure where you will go. You loved the Lord and served him all of your life, but you lost yourself and your path got foggy towards the end. I hope you can be forgiven. In the name of my Lord, Amen." Says Father Elliot in a soft voice.

"God bless you, Agnes" adds Fiona, letting a tear slip from her eyes again. They then take their spades and cover her up and flatten down the soil. Sister Agnes Kirktrut is gone for good.

Out of respect for Agnes, Father Elliot arranges a funeral type of gathering to lay Agnes to rest once and for all. Only a handful of people from the town attended. An illustration of Agnes lays by her grave alongside some lit candles. Father Elliot reads "My dear Agnes, you were one of the greatest things to ever happen to this church. Your strength, holiness and determination was inspiring. It is a great shame that you lost yourself ever so slightly towards the end of your life. But I will choose to remember you as the amazing woman I once knew you to be." He then blows out the candles and ends the ceremony.

There is something more clear about the air now. It feels as if they can breathe again. No more witches, no more attacks on the town, then the most important part for many of the people living in the town… no more evil Agnes. This evil woman, who tried to ruin everyone's lives in the name of her so called holiness, is now a thing of the past, but for sure would not be forgotten about anytime soon. But the people living in Southbrook would waste no more time in being afraid, as there was no longer anything to be afraid of, the people felt free. They still attended church, to show respect and support to Father Elliot, who they now saw as a kind hearted man, who was just perhaps scared just as scared of Agnes as they all were, hence why he left her in the hands of the witches. The town really just went back to normal. Southbrook was no longer a place that people were afraid of. Just a few weeks after the death of the witches, their coven was converted into a museum and became a large tourist attraction in the town, the church still stood and the people were simply a lot happier. Agnes' ultimate betrayal which lead to her death, was ultimately the best thing to ever happen to the town of Southbrook.

Printed in Great Britain
by Amazon